CW00410791

NEVER GO TO SEA

Since the days of Admiral Rous, the liaison between the Senior Service and the Sport of Kings has been a long and an honourable one. Slow horses have contributed just as much as fast women to the downfall of many a good naval man. It is therefore surprising that one very distinguished naval officer, none other than Commander Robert Bollinger Badger, D.S.C., R.N., known throughout the Navy as the The Artful Bodger, should reach a ripe age knowing less than a Hottentot about flat-racing. As Assistant Director of Naval Public Relations responsible for the public image of the Navy, and as part-owner of a racehorse entered in the Derby, The Bodger finds himself struggling to keep his feet in two strange worlds. Somehow the two worlds merge. Gambling everything on one chance, The Bodger attempts the most spectacular publicity coup of the century – nothing less than an assault upon the highest pinnacle of the Turf, the Blue Riband of the Epsom Derby.

Also by John Winton

WE JOINED THE NAVY

WE SAW THE SEA

DOWN THE HATCH

Never go to Sea

John Winton

Maritime Books

First published by
MICHAEL JOSEPH LTD
26 *Bloomsbury Street*
*London, W.C.*1
1963

© *copyright 1963 by John Winton*

Reprinted 2004 by
MARITIME BOOKS
Lodge Hill
Liskeard
Cornwall, PL14 4EL

'Stick close to your desks and never go to sea,
And you all may be rulers of the Queen's Navee!'

H M S Pinafore

I

The headquarters of the Ministry of Political Warfare (Admiralty Division) was a steel and concrete colossus which soared up for thirty storeys above Piccadilly, reducing Green Park by contrast to the size of a village green. The building had been constructed (at the same cost as one guided missile destroyer) to relieve the intolerable office overcrowding in Whitehall, but this admirable object had already been overtaken by events. The building had been open for six months and was now full to overflowing; two further buildings were planned, one of forty storeys in Earls Court and another of sixty storeys in Hounslow, to relieve the already intolerable office overcrowding in the new building.

Although the Ministry building had been completed for such a short time it had already become a familiar part of the London skyline and the normal traffic along Piccadilly no longer gave it a second glance. The Ministry hall porter was therefore surprised, and a little flattered, to observe through his window one morning a passer-by who appeared to be absorbed by the prospect of the outside of the Ministry of Political Warfare.

He was a burly red-faced man dressed in a dark grey suit and he had a brown trilby hat perched on top of a shock of black hair. He was standing on the edge of the pavement, his head tilted back, gazing up at the impassive canyon wall of glass and steel above him with an expression almost of awe on his face. The man's whole appearance suggested to the hall porter that he was not used to going to work in civilian clothes. The hall porter took one more look at the honest brown trilby and the suit (which itself appeared slightly abashed by the plain light of day, being more accustomed to life after dark) and concluded that the man on the pavement was a naval officer in plain clothes.

After some moments' contemplation, the figure on the pavement seemed to reach a decision, squared his shoulders, took a deep breath and advanced towards the revolving doors of the Ministry. The hall porter put away his copy of *Sporting Life* and braced himself for the encounter.

'Can I help you, Sir?'

'Yes, you can. My name is Commander Badger . . .'

'Ah yes, Commander Forster-Jones is expecting you, sir. You're the new Assistant Director, aren't you, sir?'

'That's right.'

Now that the visitor was standing so close to his desk, the hall porter experienced a prickle of memory; he felt that he ought to recognise the new Assistant Director. He took another long hard look.

'Are you the gentleman they call The Artful Bodger, sir?'

'That's right. How did you know?'

The hall porter laughed archly. 'You'd be surprised at what we know here, sir. Now if you'll just sign the book, sir, please.'

The hall porter pushed across a large book like a ledger.

'Just sign under the last name, sir, with your full name, rank and decorations.'

The Bodger looked at the previous line. 'P. FitzBeetle,' he read. '10/- to win EUROCLYDON (3.15 Redcar), any to come 10/- e.w. CAPE CANAVERAL (4.45). All S.P.'

The hall porter caught The Bodger's look of bewilderment. 'Very sorry, sir, wrong book,' he said, deftly removing the ledger and substituting another, very similar book.

The Bodger wrote carefully 'Commander Robert Bollinger Badger, DSC, RN' and pushed the book back to the hall porter.

'You a betting man, sir?'

'No, I'm afraid I don't know anything about horse-racing. It's something that's never appealed to me.'

'Ah well, if you ever feel like a little flutter, on the Derby say, you'll know where to come, sir. Settling day is Monday.'

'Thank you, but I doubt if I ever will. I'll bear it in mind though. Which floor do I go to?'

'Oh you're not on any floor, sir. You're in the basement. What we call the Kasbah, sir. Commander Forster-Jones always calls it the Truth Serum Wing, sir. Through that green baize door and down the steps and Commander Forster-Jones's office is the first on the right, sir. Shall I come with you, sir?'

'No, no, I'll find it.'

The legend on the door of the first office on the right contained comprehensive instructions for the behaviour of intending visitors. It said: 'Cdr. J. E. Forster-Jones, RN, Assistant Director of Naval Public Relations. Knock respectfully and remove your hat before entering. All except practising Buddhists may retain their shoes.'

The Bodger removed his hat, retained his shoes, knocked respectfully and went in.

'*Bodger!*'

'Hello, Jimmy!'

Jimmy Forster-Jones was perhaps The Bodger's oldest friend in the service. They had joined the Navy on the same day, relieved each other in more than one appointment and Jimmy had been The Bodger's best man. Jimmy was almost a head taller than The Bodger but stood with a perpetual stoop as though he were trying to shrug an irksome weight from his shoulders. His face was large and fleshy, like a

9

bloodhound's, and his eyes were deepset and rather mournful. The Bodger was both alarmed at his friend's weary appearance and impressed by the excellence of his suit which was of a cut far above the normal naval officer's standard (though its effect was marred by the red turban wound round Jimmy's head).

'What's the turban for, Jimmy?' The Bodger asked.

'It's not a turban, it's a wet towel. Seriously. I'm composing a rude *billet doux* for the Press Council. But come and sit down, Bodger, and tell me what you've been doing. Kick those papers off that chair there.'

The Bodger examined the pile of closely-typed papers. 'What are these?'

'Oh, there's a sort of lunatic fringe of officers who write novels in their spare time. They're supposed to send them to us for vetting. Actually they come in quite useful, as bog paper. Normally better quality than the pusser's stuff. But tell me now, what have you been doing with yourself since I last saw you. You've no *idea* how glad I am to see you, Bodger!'

'Well,' said The Bodger, 'I've just come from *Seahorse*, Britain's latest and greatest submarine . . .'

'I remember,' said Jimmy gloomily. 'I remember trying to arrange a press day for her. For some reason or other we all thought she was up in Scotland and sent the press haring off up there. They've never forgiven us for that. She was in Pompey the whole time.'

'Just as I was settling down in *Seahorse* I got promoted, of all the funny things to happen . . .'

'Yes, I heard about that, too. Congratulations.'

'But how are you, Jimmy? You look a bit shop-soiled.'

Jimmy made a despairing gesture, similar to a man clutching at a phantom straw.

'You see me almost at the end of my tether. Bodger, I

never thought I'd ever see the day when I'd be *glad* to get back to sea, but I am now. I'm just itching to get back to a normal wardroom where everyone is just normally bonkers like me.'

'I can understand that. This place looks like something out of "1984". D'you ever get any social life?'

'Not in working hours. One or two of the civil servants have the odd glass at lunchtime but watching'em at it only makes me realise what I'm missing all the more. There's nothing more blood-chilling than a civil servant trying to be sociable, Bodger. Most of them only touch alcohol at funerals, you know. Any other time they either make such an exhibition of themselves you daren't go back to that pub again or they shut up like clams and sit in a corner looking sinister. Incidentally, Bodger, before we go any further, that *suit* of yours . . .'

'Yes?' The Bodger looked fondly down at his trusty drinking suit, boon companion of many a happy evening hour.

'I should bury it,' said Jimmy firmly. 'That sort of thing is all right for the civil servants, nobody could care less if they came to work stark naked, but you and I have got a standard to keep up. I should pop round the corner and get yourself something wearable if I were you. I can give you the name of quite a decent bloke. That *hat* . . .'

'What about it?' said The Bodger defensively.

'Burn it. You mustn't be seen here in a soft hat, at least not before Goodwood, and even then it's a bit dicey.'

'I'd no idea,' said The Bodger, much chastened.

'Just a word in your ear.'

'But what about the job, Jimmy? What am I supposed to do here?'

Jimmy rubbed his chin thoughtfully. 'I don't know quite how to put this,' he said carefully. 'To cut a long story short, you're now in the Truth Serum Wing. We're the Hidden Persuaders. That's why we're hidden away in the bargain basement, the Kasbah. We're responsible for the Royal Navy's image in the eyes of the great British public. You didn't know the Navy *had* an image, did you?'

'No, I didn't,' The Bodger admitted.

'Neither did I, till I came here. We're supposed to make up what people actually think of the Navy. Everybody in the Kasbah is in some way connected with publicity for the Navy. For example, just across the passage there's old Bill Beetleson. He designs those posters saying "Join The Navy And See The World".'

'Don't tell me somebody actually *designs* those!' exclaimed The Bodger. 'I thought they just happened. They all look about fifty years old, anyway.'

'That's how long old Bill's been doing'em. Next door to him we've got George de Beetle. He writes all the Admiralty Fleet Orders . . .'

'One bloke?'

'George writes the lot. I should drop in one day and watch him at work if I were you. It's as good as a three-ring circus. Next door to him there's Frank Bethell. He's the editor of *What?*, the Royal Navy Consumer's Association magazine. He's worth a visit, too. Next door again there's Bert Beattle, the Naval Statistician. He works out why more red-headed men joined the Navy in 1931 than in any other year since 1780, and other matters of perennial interest. Then we've got Angus MacBeetle, the Sea Cadet Liaison . . .'

'Just a minute, Jimmy. Is everybody here called *Beetle?*'

Jimmy stared at The Bodger. 'Of course,' he said, at last, 'I keep forgetting you're new here, Bodger. Didn't you know that all the civil servants in the Admiralty Division are related to each other?'

'No. Are they?'

'God, yes. We've got Beetles, Bethells, Beattles, de Beetles, *van* Beetles, Beetle*sons*, Beetle*sens*, MacBeetles, FitzBeetles, we even had an Abu Ben Said Ben Hur Ben Be Atel at one time. But they're all basically beetles. You've only got to look out of the window when they're all going home at five o'clock to see how this came about. There they all are, all beetles, all beetling off to Beetaloo to catch their beetle trains to Beetle Garden City where they drink a pint of mild and betel-juice at The Three Jolly Beetles before driving home in their beetle cars to kiss their wives and beetle their eyebrows at the beetle-box all night. They're beetles all right, no doubt about it.'

'You sound a little bitter, Jimmy.'

'I've had a sickener of it all, Bodger. I'm bloody glad you're here, let me tell you. To continue. To help you in your daily struggle you've got a personal staff. There's Gwladys Beetle-Smith, your secretary. She used to be a secretary at the Foreign Office so this is a bit of a come-down for her.'

'What happened then?'

'Some unhappy love affair or other. She still gets crushes on various Foreign ministers. This week it's a Burmese. Last month it was a Venezuelan. I'm told that in Anthony Eden's day she used to go into a coma for days on end. Nobody could do a thing with her.'

'Where is she? Can I meet her?'

'She's off work today. I haven't looked in the paper but I expect there's a meeting of foreign ministers on at Geneva or something. That's always a bad time for our Gwladys. Also, you've got George Dewberry to help you, if help is the right word.'

'Now that's a familiar-sounding sort of name,' mused The Bodger.

'I'll get him.'

Jimmy pressed one of three buttons on his desk. The Bodger noted that two of them were blue and marked 'Gwladys' and 'George', and the other was red and marked 'Himself'.

'Marning, James' said a fatigued voice from somewhere overhead.

'George, you've got a hangover,' said Jimmy. 'I can hear it from here.'

'True, O king, live for ever. What can I do for you, Jimmy, this fine morning?'

'Come in and meet the new boss, George.'

'Be right with you.'

At that moment the office door opened and a face, disembodied, appeared. It was a furtive, crafty face, with a small black moustache and a sly grin.

'Heard the buzz, Jimmy? Mugsy's got the push.'

The face disappeared.

'Who on earth was that?' asked The Bodger in astonishment.

'Rodney Bethel. We call him The Tatler and Bystander. He keeps everybody up to date with the latest gossip. You can guarantee that everybody in the building knows all about *you* by now.'

'Who's Mugsy?'

Jimmy shrugged. 'Haven't the faintest idea. Some hall porter probably.'

'Has he got the sack or something?'

Jimmy shook his head decisively. 'Never. Civil servants never get the sack, Bodger. They get *reallocated* which means they turn up again in a new office next door just in time to write "Provisionally concur" on the correspondence they've just pushed out from their old office. Come in, George.'

Lieutenant George Dewberry, RN, was quite the most dissipated-looking young man The Bodger, who had some experience in these matters, had ever seen. The Bodger remembered him as one of the cadets who had passed through his hands at Dartmouth. He was not now, even in the most charitable light, a good advertisement for The Bodger's training. The Bodger remembered George Dewberry as a shy, rather tubby boy who, if The Bodger's suspicions were correct, anaesthetised himself against the rigours of his existence as a Cadet RN at Dartmouth and in the cadet training ship with periodical bouts of alcohol. Plainly he had continued the practice into later life. His suit, which was as excellently cut as Jimmy's, was strained to cover his gross figure, he walked flabbily as though any sort of physical action was an effort for him, and he wheezed heavily through his nose. However, he appeared to be glad to see The Bodger and willing to let bygones be bygones.

'Good morning, sir, we've been looking forward to you coming.'

'Good morning, George. Didn't I hear somewhere that you were retiring from the Navy, with mutual expressions of goodwill on both sides?'

George grinned. 'I was, sir. I used to slap in a letter twice a year but they were all turned down and eventually they wore me down. I shouldn't be surprised if I start working for my brass hat very soon!'

'That'll be the day,' said Jimmy. 'Why are you looking so pleased with yourself this morning, George?'

'I gotta horse! An old aunt of mine has just died and her will's just been proved. She's left me a horse.'

'Splendid, George! You'll be riding to work through Rotten Row every day.'

'Not on this horse I won't, you can bet your life! It's a

grandson of Airborne out of a Hyperion mare and it's entered for the Derby.'

'You mean a *racehorse!* What's its name?'

'Battlewagon.' George Dewberry took a letter from his pocket. 'This is a letter from my aunt's lawyers. Here it is: Battlewagon, a two-year old grey colt by Ship of the Line out of Sun of Austerlitz, by Hyperion. Ship of the Line was by Airborne out of Royal Oak, by Straight Deal,' George Dewberry added, to The Bodger.

'George, you're talking double Dutch to me,' said The Bodger.

'That's its breeding, sir. It's a pretty classily-bred horse, too. My aunt paid 3,500 guineas for it as a yearling.'

The Bodger whistled. 'That's a lot of loot for a horse, by Golly!'

'It's not *all* that much, as racehorses go, but you don't get a grandson of Airborne out of a Hyperion mare for peanuts, you know.'

'Obviously not,' said The Bodger dryly. 'Has it won any races?'

'Not that I know of, sir. My aunt bought it to run in the Derby but from what I can remember of its form, it appears she bought a pup.'

'Never mind. To get back to business a minute, what exactly do you do here, George?'

George Dewberry looked disconcerted. Jimmy hastened to fill in the embarrassed pause. 'Bodger,' he said earnestly, 'that's the one question you must *never* ask while you're here. You know the fairy story about the woodcutter's seventh son who said the magic words and the wicked magician's castle vanished? It's the same here. Ask anybody here what he's actually *doing* and the whole shooting-match will go up in smoke!'

16

'I'm very sorry, Jimmy,' said The Bodger contritely. 'I can see I've got a lot to learn.'

'I can see you have. I hardly like leaving you alone in this place. Now you'd better know something about the top boys here. You won't have much trouble with Sir James Beetleburgh, the Permanent Secretary. He's a decent old buffer. Even the other civil servants like him. *Your* main headache will be the Mekon.'

'The Mekon?'

'Ultima Thule. He lives on the thirtieth floor. The Vice Chief of Naval Staff to the Ministry of Political Warfare, otherwise known as the Director of Naval Public Relations, otherwise known as ComNavPubRep, otherwise known as Darling Richard, otherwise known as . . . well, we won't go into *that.*'

'You don't mean Richard Gilpin?'

'Himself. Rear Admiral Richard St Clair Gilpin CB, DSC, no less. He's the ideal man to look after naval publicity. You know the saying The Silent Service? He's got it tattooed on his behind. He thinks the only good publicity the Navy ever had were the notices the press gangs used to put up. Actually, it has its advantages. Naval publicity is only one of the things on his plate and you'll find that you're left very much to yourself, unless there's a question in the House or some wretched term-mate of yours gets himself into the *News of the World.* Then you'll have to hold on to your hat. Brace yourself, and we'll go and see him.'

An automatic express lift rocketed them to the top floor where, looking out of a window, The Bodger was impressed by the view of other glass and steel colossi housing other Admiralty departments. Meanwhile, Jimmy was addressing himself to a peroxide blonde secretary who was playing on a typewriter in an alcove.

'Morning, Marlene, how's the varicose veins?'

'Excruciating,' said Marlene tersely, without raising her head from the typewriter.

'Is Buddha in?'

'Yes. All on his tod.'

'Can we see him?'

'At your own risk.'

'Bless you.'

Jimmy turned to The Bodger. 'Richard's just been on a tour of the Far East and he came back with a bad attack of Buddhism.' He put his hand on the door-handle of Admiral Gilpin's office. 'Shall we dance?' he said.

The Admiral's office was a long room, thickly carpeted and in almost complete darkness except for a shaded light at one end. The Bodger had advanced almost halfway up the room behind Jimmy before he noticed that the Admiral was actually seated on top of his desk with his back to the door, his legs and arms crossed and his head bowed as though in devotion. The dim light came from a strip along the top of a gigantic map of the world which covered the wall behind the desk. The map was studded with plaques, some red with 'NUCLEAR GLOBAL' in white letters, some yellow with 'COLD WAR' in black letters, and others purple with 'LIMITED WAR' in orange letters. Obviously each plaque represented an actual or potential war zone and The Bodger was appalled by their numbers and their distribution. According to Admiral Gilpin's map, there was hardly a spot on the seething globe, from the Falkland Islands to the Arctic Circle and from Fiji to Madagascar, where some kind of war was not either in progress or imminent. The Bodger had been in the habit of reading his daily newspaper and concluding that the world seemed to be rubbing along in the same old way. Now he realised that he, along with the rest of the world, was apparently reading his newspaper on top of an active volcano.

Admiral Gilpin's meditations were not so deep that he was unaware of their approach.

'Yes?' The Admiral maintained his attitude of devotion; indeed the whole interview was conducted by him in the same position.

'Forster-Jones, sir. May I introduce my relief, Commander Badger, sir?'

'Are you going, Jones?'

'Yes, sir!'

'And you're taking over, Badger?'

'Yes, sir.'

'Well, Badger, I'll say to you what I said to Jones when he first came here.' The Admiral raised his head and seemed to be studying some minor conflagration in the region of the Yangstse river. 'The idea seems to have grown up in recent years – it's only a very recent idea – that the Navy needs publicity. In my opinion this is pure unadulterated bunkum! I know you agree with me, Jones.'

'Yes, sir,' Jimmy replied dutifully.

'We've had a Navy for something like a thousand years and only in the last few decades has anyone thought of giving it *publicity!*' The Admiral emphasised the last word as though he were referring to a particularly loathsome disease. 'We're not selling stockings, we're not trying to make money, we're not trying to make the public think we're *good chaps*, we've got our own job to do and it's no damn business of anyone else how we do it! Right?'

'Right, sir,' said Jimmy.

'However, it was decided a few years ago, at a very high level, that the Navy should have an image. Having decided that the Navy should have an image it was then decided that that image should be preserved. The fact that nobody has yet decided what the Navy's image should *be* is neither here nor there. In my opinion, there is only one image for the Navy. The Silent Service! Silent in word and deed, particularly in word. I expect you to preserve that image, Badger. If you decide to suppress any story or any particulars of a story you can count on my fullest support. Work on the principle of a "Need to Know" and you can take it that the press need to know nothing! The less they know the better. That's true isn't it?'

'Sir,' said Jimmy.

'I only wish you could suppress all so-called naval correspondents and their newspapers too. Very well. Good-bye, Badger. I don't expect to see you again until you yourself are relieved. Good-bye, Jones.'

'Good-bye, sir.'

Once outside the Admiral's office, Jimmy crossed quickly to Marlene's alcove and kicked her wastepaper basket ten feet.

'Sometimes,' he said to The Bodger, 'I wish somebody would promote that man to Pope. At least then we'd only have to kiss his ring.'

2

Jimmy Forster-Jones preserved a morose silence until he reached his own office again.

'There's not much more to tell you now, Bodger,' he said, 'except the domestic details. The teaboat comes round at ten-thirty in the morning and three-thirty in the afternoon. It'll cost you half-a-crown a week. The Kasbah cat's name is Tibbles. She's expecting again in the next fortnight sometime. There's a big black tom from the Ministry of Ag. and Fish who periodically rapes her. Frank Bethell runs the department football pool syndicate. That costs half-a-crown a week, too. I only joined it because it would have been insufferable if they'd won something one week and I wasn't in on it. They never did, incidentally. The best pub in these parts is The Vaults, just around the corner from here. They make pretty good ham sandwiches too. The local bookmaker's name is Traddle. The hall porter will always get your money on for you but if you want to get in touch with the man himself you can do it through Tommy Spares, the barber at the back of this building. Tommy's is a useful hide-out if the pace gets too hot some time and you want to keep out of the way for a little while. And that's about all, I think. Well, got the weight, Bodger?'

'I suppose so.'

'Right.' Jimmy fitted his bowler hat carefully on his head and took up his umbrella and his copy of *The Times*. 'Last time I'll need these, I hope. I'll say good-bye then and leave you to it. Good-bye Bodger, and the best of public relations luck. You'll need it.'

'Thank you, Jimmy.'

The door slammed shut. Jimmy was gone. The Bodger was firmly in the chair of the Assistant Director of Naval Public Relations.

The Bodger examined his new office. The room was barely furnished, almost spartan. There was the desk on which were a tray full of pencils, rubbers and paper clips; the office intercom – the Squawk Box; a GPO telephone; an internal Ministry exchange telephone; a board on which Jimmy had scribbled useful telephone numbers; a telephone directory; and two or three ashtrays filled with stubs. On the wall to The Bodger's right hung a chart representing a calendar for the year, with the months, weeks and days ruled off in squares; someone had coloured in the dates which concerned the Naval Public Relations Department – red for Navy Days and flying display days, blue for the Royal Tournament and exhibitions at Olympia, green for visits of HM Ships to the Pool of London, yellow for dates on which HM Ships were due to commission or launch, and purple for Aintree, Epsom, Royal Ascot and Goodwood. On The Bodger's left was a tall bookcase, put together from lengths of rough deal planking, crammed with newspapers, magazines, folders and assorted books. On top of the bookcase lay a large scrapbook. The Bodger took it down and carried it back to his desk.

The scrapbook was marked The Black Book and it was a compendium of all the private nightmares of a public relations man. In it Jimmy Forster-Jones had pasted all the stories which must have caused him to moan restlessly in his sleep. The Bodger turned over the pages. The headlines sprang to his eye. NEW NAVY CARRIER AGROUND OFF PORT-

LAND: SHAMBLES BUOY SHAMBLES; 'Bound to happen,' says A.B. EXPLOSION IN HUSH NAVY PLANT: SABOTAGE? 'All a busted flush,' says A.B. WRENS NEW NIGHTIE COMPLAINT: 'Indecent,' says Commandant, 'Smashing,' says A.B.

'Who the devil is this A.B. they keep quoting?' The Bodger muttered.

Some of the stories were accompanied by ominous slips from Admiral Gilpin. 'Jones: *What* is all this about?', 'Jones: Come and see me *immediately*' and 'Jones: *Who* was responsible for this?'

Dispersed among the headline stories were articles about the Navy. These, The Bodger soon discovered, were far more deadly than the headlines. They were all feature articles, written by special correspondents who were skilled craftsmen. Each one was a calculated blend of observed fact, intelligent guesswork, reported hearsay, and unabashed fabrication. Each one was diabolically beautiful, the words falling into place as remorselessly as the drops of a Chinese torture. Each one slid into The Bodger's heart like a rapier.

'. . . From my hotel window I can still see the tall plume of black smoke rising from the heat-blackened debris which is all that remains this morning of the Navy's new £50m. guided weapon . . .'

'. . . There were red faces at Admiralty House this morning when the latest recruiting figures were published. "What happened?" I asked bluff, hearty Admiral Sir Seamus Dogpit (54) . . .'

'. . . Do we need a Navy? "Why can't you fellows stick to football matches" retorted slim, ascetic Admiral Gilpin (47), wartime destroyer veteran, when I asked him this very question . . .'

The Bodger read on with a sinking heart. Each successive thrust was more wounding than the last. The Bodger read of collisions, groundings, fire at sea, grave insubordination, courts martial, boards of enquiry, sailors being committed to gaol, officers being cited as co-respondents – all the scores of domestic and professional tragedies which were the Navy's lot during an average year were outlined in an unforgiving spotlight. It seemed that the most recent naval occasion to receive a favourable notice in the British press had been the engagement off Cape Trafalgar. The Bodger despondently returned the Black Book to the shelf and at the same time noticed a modestly-sized folder which had been partly obscured by the Black Book. The folder was labelled The Happy Pack. The Bodger carried it back to his desk as tenderly as he would have borne a bundle of old love letters.

The first few pages of the Happy Pack were enough to show The Bodger that, compared with the Black Book, the Happy Pack was pitched on a markedly minor key. The cuttings in the Black Book had been taken from national newspapers with daily circulations of three million or more. The Happy Pack's sources, on the other hand, were regional and local organs with weekly circulations of three thousand or less.

ST ALBANS GIRL WEDS SAILOR. The Bodger noted that the bride had been given away by her father and that the honeymoon was to be spent in the Channel Islands; the accompanying photograph of the happy couple revealed the bridegroom, obviously a Chief Stoker, leering at the camera with an expression of newly-found nuptial rapture. The rest of the Happy Pack's stories were similarly heart-warming. WARTIME SUB HERO OPENS FLOWER SHOW. LIGHT-HOUSE KEEPER RELIEVED BY NAVY 'COPTER. NEW NAAFI OPEN AT LLANPUMPSAINT: 'Not bad,' says A.B.

'That bloody A.B. again,' said The Bodger viciously.

Just as The Bodger was finishing the Happy Pack, the telephone rang.

'Good morning, Amalgamated Press Bureau here,' said the voice at the other end, briskly.

'Oh yes?' said The Bodger blankly.

'We've just had a report that the Navy are going to build twelve more nuclear submarines in the next ten years . . .'

'Wish we were,' said The Bodger.

'Have you any comment to make on this?'

'If it's true, which I doubt, I'd say it was a very good thing. Lot better than building all those damn great useless carriers.'

'That's not Jimmy Forster-Jones speaking, surely?' The voice sounded incredulous.

'No, it's The Bodger. His relief.'

'Pleased to meet you, Bodger. You've just taken over Jimmy's job?'

'Yes.'

'Best of luck then.'

'Thank you.'

'Still talking about this report, do you think we can afford twelve nuclears?'

'Bloody certain we can't! But we could if we built a few less offices and a few more ships.'

'*Really*,' said the voice. 'I must say that never occurred to me.' The voice fairly oozed friendliness. Whoever was speaking obviously had spent his life on the telephone.

'Who am I speaking to?' The Bodger asked.

'Jim Sewter, Naval Correspondent for the Amalgamated Press Bureau. Tell me, Bodger, why have they suddenly switched to nuclears like this . . .'

The Bodger gave his views at length. Jim Sewter listened attentively and, when The Bodger had finished, thanked him sincerely. The Bodger eventually put down the telephone with a comfortable feeling of satisfaction. His first essay into public relations had gone off very well. If this was the sort of thing which had given Jimmy that hunted look then The Bodger could only suppose that his old friend had been an incipient neurotic all his life.

The Bodger decided it was time he looked round his department. He recalled that Jimmy had said that Frank Bethell, the Editor of *What?* the Royal Navy Consumer's Association publication, was well worth a visit. Behind the door marked RNCA *What?* The Bodger could hear the labouring of breath, the padding of feet and the thuds of heavy bodies being thrown about. It sounded very much as though Frank Bethell was using his office as a part-time gymnasium. The Bodger knocked and opened the door.

A laboratory bench littered with glass containers, instruments and electrical cables ran the length of one side of Frank Bethell's office. Facing the bench were several machines among which The Bodger recognised a lathe, a hydraulic press and a very large microscope. Across the room three stout steel wire ropes were stretched between metal posts which The Bodger identified as standard guard-rail stanchions in regular use in HM Ships. Against these wires a red-bearded man dressed in a padded waistcoat and a crash helmet was hurling himself, falling to the floor, picking himself up, and launching himself yet again. The office floor shook at each fall. The red-bearded man swore volubly. Clouds of dust rose up.

Just as the bearded man was winding himself up for yet another assault, he caught sight of The Bodger.

'Hah!' he cried. 'You must be the new Assistant Director!'

'That's right.'

The waistcoated figure uncoiled himself and stood upright revealing himself as a huge man, a full head and shoulders taller than The Bodger. He weighed, The Bodger estimated, at least seventeen stone and his face was flattened and crushed, like a pugilist's. His red beard gave him a rakish, piratical appearance. He and The Bodger shook hands. When The Bodger had recovered the use of that hand, he motioned towards the guardrails.

'What's happening here?'

'Just doing a consumer test on guardrails, old boy. Seeing what they'll stand up to.'

'But we've had that sort for years!'

'About time we did a test on 'em, eh?'

'They don't get that sort of treatment at sea, you know.'

'At sea? At sea? Who cares what happens at sea!' Frank Bethell cried jovially.

'Oh, I'm sorry,' said The Bodger. 'I thought you were testing stuff to go into ships.'

'Ships? *Ships?*' Frank Bethell gave a rollicking piratical guffaw. 'They're only a *very* small part of our work. There's far more of the Navy ashore than afloat, you know that. The last test we ran for *that* side of the Navy was on weed killers . . .'

'*Weed killers!* You needn't tell me you need *weed killer* in ships!'

'Don't you just! You obviously haven't seen the Reserve Fleet lately. Why, they used to get two crops of hay a year from *Elephant's* flight deck before she went to the breakers. And as for *Carousel*, that ship was a floating Kew Gardens. Not a word of a lie. There was a young *beech tree* growing outside the wireless office, mustard and cress in every mess-deck, and mushrooms in all the bilges. You won't believe me, but in today's Navy there are more ships using weed killer than there are using fuel oil!'

Although The Bodger had a suspicion that Frank Bethell was not exaggerating, he refused to allow himself to be depressed and indeed went back to his office pleased with his new department and looking forward to the future as to an exciting challenge.

The Bodger's buoyant mood lasted until just after lunch when The Tatler and Bystander poked his head round The Bodger's office door, said 'Somebody's in trouble', and vanished again. He was immediately followed by George Dewberry, reeking of best bitter and carrying a bundle of newspapers.

'Sir, sir, have you seen these?'

'No? What's the trouble, the favourite beaten in the two-thirty?'

The Squawk Box on The Bodger's desk hummed and crackled. '*Badger!*'

The Bodger fumbled with the switch. 'Yes, sir?'

'It seems my words fell on stony ground this morning. I require your reasons in writing on my desk before nine o'clock tomorrow morning.'

'Aye aye, sir.'

The Bodger seized one of the newspapers. 'What *is* all this about, George, for God's sake?'

'Front page, sir.'

The Bodger smoothed the paper out on his desk. He had no difficulty in finding the cause of the trouble. Under the headline NAVY TO GET TWELVE ATOM SUBS: FURORE IN WHITE-HALL, The Bodger read: 'The news that the Navy is to get twelve nuclear submarines during the next ten years has touched off the biggest Whitehall row in years, official Admiralty sources confirmed this morning. The announcement is regarded as an official rebuke to the present Admiralty carrier building programme. The new plan is described as "irresponsible" by several commentators. "We can't afford them" was the official view of an Admiralty spokesman this morning. The twelve subs (work is expected to start on them early next year) are also causing concern in the building industry. It is understood that several contracts for government buildings have been cancelled to provide the money for the submarines. Mr Ben Hodder, General Secretary of the Amalgamated Bricklayers' and Road-Hauliers' Union, described the latest Admiralty move as "a stab in the back" . . .'

With a sick feeling of horror, The Bodger recognised his own words on the telephone that morning running like a thread through the story but so blown out of shape and proportion, so hideously distorted, that they might have been reflected through a devilishly-warped mirror.

'There's a leading article on page six, sir,' said George Dewberry.

The leader commented bitterly on the front page story, embellishing the bare news, hinting that the submarine v. carrier storm had weakened the Navy to a state of feeble debility unequalled since de Ruyter appeared in the Medway, implying that corruption was now rife in the Navy to an extent unsurpassed since the days of the fourth Earl of Sandwich, and ending on a clarion call – 'What would Nelson have said?'

'What *would* Nelson have said,' The Bodger echoed. He sat back in his chair and swallowed. Then a slow cold rage possessed him.

'That dirty . . . double-crossing . . . two-faced . . . little *twister*,' he gritted through clenched teeth.

'Who was it, sir?' asked George Dewberry.

'A cesspit called Jim Sewter. *Sewer* would be more accurate!'

'What exactly did you tell him, sir?'

'Oh, I spoke in very general terms, that I thought the new submarines were a good idea if we could afford them and so on. I see now that I said far too much and that . . . that slimy *coyote* was taking it all down to be used in evidence against me. You know, George, I've never trusted the press. I've had one or two brushes with them in the past and I thought I knew how to deal with them. Obviously I've got a great deal still to learn. And he was so *polite*, too, God blast his eyes!'

'They always are, sir,' said George Dewberry, gloomily.

'Well, that does it George. I won't be caught napping again. By God, I'll be on my toes from now on! Any stupid little reporter who tries to buttonhole me after this will get a thick ear, I can tell you!'

'I shouldn't worry too much about this, sir. It's always happening. There'll be some new sensation tomorrow and everybody will have forgotten all about it, sir. You'll see.'

'But this was deliberate, inflammatory *distortion!*' The Bodger thumped his fist on his desk in an agony of frustration. 'Deliberate! What have they got against the Navy anyway? Anybody would think we'd murdered their grandmothers or something!'

George Dewberry cleared his throat and coughed tactfully. 'One thing I've learnt since I've been here, if you don't mind my mentioning it, sir, is that the best way to treat the press is as businessmen. Their business is after all to sell their newspapers, sir, and they're not too particular how they do it. I just don't believe they're either pro-Navy or anti-Navy, sir. There *may* be one or two screwballs amongst them who genuinely hate the Navy and would love to do it down, but most of them give me the impression they're not interested in the Navy at all except when it provides them with a story. The rest of the time they couldn't care less about the Navy one way or the other. The reason they always report the bad news so well is simply because bad news is always the best news. Everybody enjoys reading about a really juicy disaster, sir, and the fact that it happens to us once in a while is just our horrible luck. It's a fundamental human thing, sir. Lots of people from Dante downwards have made bloody good shots at describing what Hell is going to be like, but nobody, not even Dante, has ever succeeded in making Heaven sound interesting.'

The Bodger smiled. 'Bless you, George,' he said warmly. 'That's the first *sane* thing anybody's said to me today!'

3

'George,' The Bodger said into the Squawk Box the next morning, 'can you tear yourself away from the runners and riders at Newmarket for a minute?'

'Be right with you, sir.'

The Bodger had never concerned himself with what people thought about the Navy. His business had always been to serve in it and let others worry about selling it. But now that he was Assistant Director of Naval Public Relations it had suddenly become very much his business to worry about what people thought of the Navy. The Bodger had sent for the Department's most recent press cutting files and set to work to examine the efforts of his predecessors in the Department.

The press cuttings confirmed the impression left by Jimmy Forster-Jones' Black Book. The last major naval occasion to receive a favourable press had been the recent engagement off Cape Trafalgar. When The Bodger came across a closely-reasoned and profusely foot-noted article from a weekly paper which proved that the Battle of Trafalgar had actually been a victory for the French, The Bodger gave a bellow of exasperation and hurled the file across the office into the wastepaper basket.

'As I see it,' he said to George Dewberry, 'we all ought to be damned grateful to the man on the Player's packet. He's provided the only consistently good publicity the Navy's ever had!'

'It sometimes looks that way, sir,' said George Dewberry.

'We've had something like three thousand press cuttings here over the last six months or so and well over two thousand of them are what I would call bad. An aircraft carrier is refitted at a cost of five million pounds and can't complete her trials programme because her catapults are defective. A guided missile control system is abandoned after development costs of *fourteen million*. And why? Because some bright boffin somewhere took it into his head to tot up the final dimensions one day and said "Guess what? It's going to be too big to go into the ship!" '

George Dewberry shrugged. 'It doesn't surprise me, sir.'

'It wouldn't be so bad if the *good* stories were correspondingly big. But they're not. A Lady Mayoress visits a new frigate and is very impressed with the sailor's living accommodation. Four sailors in various parts of the country leap into various stretches of water and rescue children from drowning. A petty officer wins a safe driving contest in Hull. And so on.'

'I often think that sort of small good item does more good than the big bad item does harm, sir. The general public doesn't know much about carriers and catapults and guided weapon systems and what they cost. A few more millions more or less doesn't worry many people. But they do know all about Lady Mayoresses and children drowning and safe driving contests.'

'That's a very good point, George. That hadn't occurred to me.'

'You've got to remember I've heard all this before from Jimmy, sir,' said George Dewberry, modestly.

The Bodger grinned. 'I'm sure you have, George. But bear with me a minute. The most serious thing about it is that in all these press cuttings I can't find one story, one release, which looks as though it has originated from this department. Here we've got this *enor*mous department, *crammed* with bodies, all working *flat out*, and between them they didn't come up with one solitary idea for giving the Navy a chuck-up! There's going to be some changes, George, I can promise you,' said The Bodger grimly.

'Jimmy used to have a meeting every now and again and give them all a pep-talk.'

The Bodger shook his head emphatically. 'That doesn't do the slightest bit of good. I know how these fellows' minds work. Whenever any serving officer tries to chivvy up the civil servants they just dig their heels in, withdraw all their papers, and wait for the awkward bloke to be relieved. They've got the whip hand and they know it. If they run up against an officer who's difficult they know they've only got to hang on for a couple of years and he'll move on to another job, and what's two years in a place like this, where a thousand ages in their sight are like an evening gone? The new bloke is bound to be more amenable if only because he won't know what the hell's going on for at least the first year. No, we've got to do good by stealth. If only we could find out what the average person *really* thought about the Navy ... I wonder if we could do something on the lines of that house-to-house questioning business, sort of gallup poll approach ... Why are you looking like that, George?'

George Dewberry was gazing up at the ceiling with an expression of patient resignation on his face.

'I knew you'd get around to that idea eventually, sir. It was a thought Jimmy had when he first got here. "George," he said to me, "I need someone to do some nose-counting. You've been chosen from thousands of applicants. I want you to hop round the local borough and find out what Mrs Great Britain thinks about *her* Navy ..." '

'Well?'

'Well sir, I put on my most sociable manner, knocked on the first door and asked the first Mrs Great Britain what she thought of the Royal Navy. She said she never used the stuff and shut the door in me face. The next one said I'd have to wait until her husband got home that night. The third asked me how much the first down payment was. The fourth good lady told me to wait a minute, went and fetched her handbag, gave me half a crown and shut the door. I never saw the fifth old hag at all. She slipped her man-eating Alsatian from a sort of starting-gate by the back door and I left with one bound over the hedge, minus a large piece of trouser leg. And that was that. We never tried it again.'

'I see,' said The Bodger. He frowned thoughtfully. 'There's no doubt that the Navy gets its best publicity during wars and revolutions. I don't suppose there's a chance of one of those, is there?'

'No, sir. Things are pretty quiet at the moment, war and revolution-wise. We seem to have struck a calm patch.'

'You wouldn't think so, if you judged by the Admiral's map. According to that we're in action the whole time, all singing and dancing. As it is, we haven't even got an earthquake we can provide relief for. That's always good for a front-page picture and a story.'

'You're beginning to think like a public relations man already, sir!'

'My God, am I?' The Bodger, aghast. 'I must watch that.'

'Would you like to meet some professional advertising men, sir? They're always good at making smoke without fire. I know a couple who use The Vaults.'

'That's a splendid suggestion, George. We'll do just that.' The Bodger pressed the Squawk Box button for Gwladys. (Gwladys, when at last she put in an appearance at the office, was a large dreamy-eyed brunette who had given The Bodger one appraising look and then, apparently deciding that he was unlikely ever to become a Foreign Minister, more or less ignored him.)

'Gwladys, I'm just going out to The Vaults for lunch. Be back at two.'

'Very good, sir,' said Gwladys's voice listlessly.

'What's the matter with Gwladys today, George?'

'The disarmament conference is on again. She spends all her time staring at the bulkhead, probably dreaming of the day some handsome young Foreign Secretary will swoop down and carry her off in his briefcase.'

The Vaults was a brisk five minutes' walk (by George Dewberry) away. The Bodger took to the place at once. It was a pub which had so far escaped the ravishes of the re-decorators and remained much as it had been for the last sixty years. The engraved glasswork on the mirror behind the bar, the oak partitions which divided the bar into sections, the smell of beer and the dark comfortable interior still preserved the atmosphere which had once concerned worthy Victorian ladies with the morals of the lower drinking classes. The Vaults had no pretensions. It existed to sell beer and spirits and it expected its clientele to consume beer and spirits as fast as they could while they were on the premises and to leave decently when they had consumed enough. George Dewberry was evidently well-known there; the bar-maid had taken down a quart pewter tankard from the hook behind the bar and filled it with best bitter before he had finished removing his coat.

George Dewberry ran an expert eye over the customers. 'He's here,' he said to The Bodger. 'Just the man we want.'

George Dewberry's friend wore an air of flashy prosperity. He was the sort of man The Bodger imagined would thrive while the nation was booming but would vanish like a swallow in winter during a slump. His windsor knot was tied a little too spaciously, his shirt collar points were a little too widely separated, his shoes were a little too narrow and his trouser bottoms a little too tapered, but The Bodger recognised an expert in the trade and prepared to be polite.

'Geoff, I'd like you to meet my new boss,' George Dewberry was saying. 'Commander Badger, Geoffrey Pinner, sir.'

'Morning, Cap'n, pleased to meet yer.'

'How do you do?' said The Bodger.

'What are you drinking, Geoff?'

'Large whisky, if it's all the same to you, George. What's this, your birthday or something?'

'We want some gen on advertising, Geoff.'

'You've come to the right shop, matie! What can I do for you?'

George Dewberry looked at The Bodger.

'One of the things we want to know,' The Bodger began, 'is how you go about finding what people want to buy ...'

'Aha!' cried Geoff Pinner. 'Now you've asked the most difficult thing of all! If I knew that I'd be a millionaire. One thing I can tell you. You won't find out what makes people tick by asking them. People are funny, see. They're funnier than you think. Ask a man a question straight out and he'll do one of two things. He'll tell you what he thinks *you* think he ought to think. Or he'll be honest and tell you what he *thinks* he thinks. But neither of them will be what he *really* thinks. You got to dig deep, see, real deep, you got to turn him inside out and find out what he's really thinking, deep down inside. And you've got to do it without him knowing it. Ever tried to sell lavatory pans?'

'No, I haven't,' The Bodger confessed.

Geoff Pinner sucked his breath sharply between his teeth. 'Murder. Pure murder. You can't even show 'em on the advertisement. Call 'em lavatory pans, which is what they *are* and everybody knows it, and you'll go bust. Call 'em toilet receptacles and you'll make a million. Then there's other things. Things you wouldn't expect . . .'

Geoff Pinner drained his glass and looked expectantly at The Bodger. The Bodger caught the barmaid's eye.

'Give you an example. A year ago a firm that makes motorboats decided there was a demand for a new speedboat. They did some market research and everybody told 'em they'd love to own a new speedboat. We handled their account and we put out a beautiful ad. Had everything. Blue water, sunny day, palm trees, red boat goin' about fifty knots, clouds of spray, lovely girl in a bikini with her hair streaming behind her, water-skiing. Everything. Boat had a fibre-glass hull, choice of four colours, built-in buoyancy tanks, dozens of extras, fifty bhp outboard motor, very reasonable price. Lovely boat. Lovely ad. And what happened? *What happened?*'

Geoff Pinner looked straight at The Bodger.

'*I* don't know,' said The Bodger, despite himself.

'Flop. Flop from way back. Couldn't move 'em off the floor. Nobody wanted to know. So, we went into this, find out what went wrong, like. Everything ·was there, why wasn't the stuff moving? When we found out, we could've kicked ourselves. We should've known, a firm with our experience . . .'

'What was the *trouble?*' The Bodger demanded, unable to contain his impatience. Whatever his other faults, Geoff Pinner was a raconteur approaching genius.

'It was the wives. They didn't like the angle the boat was tilting up at. Thought it wasn't safe. Most of all they didn't like the girl in the bikini. *We* thought they'd project themselves as the girl in the bikini. You got to *project*, see? Not *likely* they didn't project themselves as the girl in the bikini! That girl wasn't them, it was the fast little bird their husband was going to pick up to go with the boat when their back was turned, see.'

'So what did you do?'

'Scrapped it. Started again. This time we kept the blue water and the palm trees but we showed the boat from the driver's angle, the cockpit, the steering wheel, all the controls, courtesy mirror on the windscreen, handbag in the glove locker and a little blue silk flag flying out front. That did it. Can't make 'em fast enough now. What are you pushing?'

'The Navy,' said George Dewberry quickly.

'The Navy! The Royal Navy?'

'Yes.'

Geoff Pinner grimaced. 'That's tough. What part of the Navy?'

'All of it.'

'Yeah, but what's the angle? What are you trying to make people do, buy it, wear it, or give it away as a present?'

'Join it.'

Geoff Pinner grimaced again. 'First thing you want to do is sack that clunkhead who designs your posters. I seen some of his stuff. That kind of approach is strictly from the Stone Age. But before you start going to town on this you got to remember one thing. Advertising will only take you so far. After that you got to *produce*. Join the Navy and see the world. Once he's joined, you got to *show* him the world. Join the Navy for a life of adventure. You got to *give* him a life of adventure. 'Cos all these recruits you get have all got kid brothers and if you're a kid who's keen on joining the

Navy all the advertising in the world won't make up for a big brother who's *in* the Navy and clouts your head every time you mention it.'

The Bodger saw that perhaps he had been too hasty in judging Geoff Pinner; beneath the effervescent froth of language ran still layers of real wisdom. 'What actually happens once he's in is beyond our province,' he said. 'Our job is to get them in.'

'*Well*, never mind,' said Geoff Pinner generously, 'mebbe I *can* give you a few ideas . . .'

*　　　　*　　　　*

The Bodger came away from The Vaults in thoughtful mood.

George Dewberry was apologetic. 'I'm sorry he was a bit overpowering, sir, but it *is* his job . . .'

'Good heavens George, don't be ridiculous! I learned the devil of a lot from all that. I must pay a social call on old Bill Beetleson . . .'

The Bodger found Bill Beetleson at his easel, just putting the finishing dabs to a portrait of a young sailor. It was an ingenuous face, smiling diffidently from the canvas, and The Bodger might have been impressed by its recruiting qualities had he not observed more than fifty replicas of the same face hanging round the walls of Bill Beetleson's office. In one poster the face smiled from a background of an antique four-funnelled destroyer pitching into a heavy sea. The head appeared again, smiling from a painting of a Swordfish landing on HMS *Furious*, and a third showed him smiling from what appeared to be the gangway of a nuclear submarine. Bill Beetleson painted the same picture twice a year. The background changed with the times but the face was eternal.

'What's the background going to be this time, Bill?' The Bodger asked.

Bill Beetleson got up from his stool and stood back to look at his work. 'I don't know. I thought I might do a view of HMS *Victory*, dressed over-all. What d'you think?'

'Not very original, is it?'

The Bodger noticed the quick concern spring into Bill Beetleson's eyes. Bill was a nice old boy and The Bodger was anxious not to hurt his feelings.

'What I meant was, could we try some other sort of picture?'

Bill Beetleson gazed at The Bodger uncomprehendingly. 'But we *always* do this kind!'

'I know, Bill.' Sometimes The Bodger thought that Bill Beetleson would have been excellently cast as a gentleman of the Deep South: he had the silver hair and kindly eyes which went well with magnolia trees, molasses, and a wife from Old Virginny. The Bodger could just picture Bill Beetleson sipping mint juleps, being polite to the uncouth Federal soldiery and philanthropic towards his slaves.

'Would you mind if I had a go at this, Bill?'

'You mean painting posters?'

'Not actually paint them but design some new ones. It won't affect your work. I just want to try out some new ideas.'

'By all means,' Bill Beetleson said, unhappily. 'Shall I carry on with this one?'

'Good heavens yes. I might not have any success at all.'

The Bodger summoned into conference Ted Beetlebotham and Danny Beetelsen, the department's photography and layout experts, and explained his ideas. After years of working with Bill Beetleson and taking photographs for instruction manuals they were both only too anxious to fall in with The Bodger's suggestions; indeed they rapidly became too enthusiastic, and The Bodger was forced to dampen some of their most flamboyant suggestions. After a week's hard work and argument The Bodger felt that he had half a dozen worthwhile ideas.

'We'll try these for a start,' he said, 'and see how they go. Send them to different parts of the country and compare results.'

The Bodger allocated the new posters to various parts of the British Isles and sat back, confident that a new era in naval recruiting advertising had dawned. He did not have to wait long for results. The first man to ring up was the Recruiting Officer (N.E. Area).

'I want to speak to whoever's responsible for this new recruiting poster.'

'That's me,' said The Bodger, touched that the man had taken the trouble to ring him up personally.

'You ought to be ashamed of yourself! What do you mean by it?'

'What do I mean by *what?*' replied The Bodger, needled by the man's tone.

'This new *poster*, confound it! I've got my office door locked at the moment! There's a queue half a mile long outside! What was the matter with the *old* poster? That brought me in a steady two candidates a week. I could handle that. But *this*, this is impossible. What do you mean by "The Navy Is All Things To All Men"?'

'We thought it a very effective slogan,' said The Bodger smoothly.

'*Effective!*' The Recruiting Officer (N.E. Area) choked. The Bodger could hear him struggling to control his paroxysm. 'I've got every queer and nancy-boy north of the Tees outside my office at the moment! Is that the sort of public you're aiming for?'

'I see what you mean,' said The Bodger. 'You mean the poster has been misunderstood?'

'*Misunderstood!*'

'Perhaps we had better withdraw it?'

'Perhaps we better had,' retorted the Recruiting Officer breathlessly and hung up.

The Bodger put down his telephone. It rang again immediately. It was the Recruiting Officer (S.W. Area) enquiring about the new recruiting poster.

'Is this a joke or something, because if it is then I don't see it. We're recruiting officers, you know, not flogging laxatives . . .'

'*Eh?*' shouted The Bodger.

'What's all this about "Be Regular in A Man's Navy"?'

'Say that again?'

'That's what it says. Be Regular in A Man's Navy. I found a bag of prunes on my office doorstep this morning . . .'

'It seems to be a printer's error. It should read "Be *A* Regular in a Man's Navy".'

'*Now* you tell me!'

'I really am most terribly sorry,' said The Bodger apologetically. 'The proofs were certainly quite all right when they left here. You'd better withdraw that poster . . .'

'I already have,' said the Recruiting Officer (S.W. Area) indignantly and rang off. This time The Bodger did not put down his telephone but kept the receiver in his hand and was rewarded by the deep mellow contralto tones of the Director of WRNS Recruiting, First Officer Matilda Grundy.

'Is that you, Bodger?'

'Hello, Matty. How's the old salt mine?'

'No time for flippancy, dear. Have . . . you . . . seen . . . the . . . new . . . *Vogue?*'

'I haven't had a chance yet. You mean the new Wrens recruiting advertisement?'

'I mean the new Wrens recruiting advertisement.'

The Bodger remembered it well. It was a glossy photograph of a pretty redhead in Wren's uniform standing in a Piccadilly traffic jam. The caption The Bodger had thought particularly telling – 'I Dreamed I Stopped The Traffic In My Wren's Uniform'.

'What's the matter, didn't we get the uniform right?' he asked. 'Stockings not straight?'

'*Ho!*' hooted Matty. 'The uniform's all right. What there is of it!'

A nightmare fear momentarily bypassed The Bodger's heart beats.

'Isn't she wearing the uniform?'

'Only the hat.'

'*Nothing else?*' shrieked The Bodger.

'Not a stitch, dear.'

'Oh dear, oh dear,' moaned The Bodger. 'Oh dear, oh dear. I suppose this will foul up your recruiting for years.'

'On the contrary, dear, it's a wow! Business has never been better! The trouble *is*, it isn't bringing us in *quite* the type of gel we want, if you see what I mean. I'm afraid I shall have to kill it, Bodger. It's a pity, but there.'

'Oh dear, oh dear,' The Bodger repeated.

'You know, you really shouldn't do these things, Bodger.'

'But Matty!' The Bodger protested wildly. 'I swear honest to God, the whole thing's a mistake! Just wait till I get my hands on that photographer!'

Matty chuckled. 'Stow it, Bodger. I know you. Tell that to the Marines. Better still, tell it to the Wrens!'

The Bodger took out his handkerchief and dabbed his brow. The morning which had promised to be such a triumph had turned out to be a nightmare. When The Bodger's telephone rang again he sprang at it like a caged panther.

'Recruiting Officer for Wales here. What is the meaning of this poster I have before me? I was hardly able to meet the Reverend Morgan's eye in chapel last Sunday. Evans, he said to me, so it's the Navy descending to primitive symbolism, is it? And if that was not bad enough, he preached his sermon on John, four, forty-eight. Except ye see signs and wonders, ye will not believe . . .'

'Just a minute, just a minute,' The Bodger put in testily. He could remember the Welsh poster quite distinctly. It was a beautifully evocative colour photograph of Trafalgar Square at dawn on a summer morning. Nelson's column was silhouetted against a pearly sky and the unexceptionable caption was: 'Are *You* Good Enough for Nelson?'

'The picture is only Trafalgar Square, you know,' said The Bodger.

'They don't know that in the valleys. *Phallic* it is, man. I have torn up this heathen offering with my own hands. Good-bye.'

'Good-bye,' said The Bodger dejectedly. He was so cast down by the unexpected hostile reaction to his new posters that the complaints of the Recruiting Officer (N.W. Area) ('They Laughed When I Joined The Navy – But You Should See Me Now') and of the Recruiting Officer (Midlands) ('The Navy – For People Who Can't Brush Their Teeth After Every Meal!') hardly registered upon his mind. He was however roused by the attack on his own favourite, his choice for London and the Home Counties.

The poster was a full length portrait in colour of The Bodger himself wearing a black eyepatch over his left eye and dressed in his No. 1 uniform with sword and medals.

He was standing against a background of draped red velvet and the simple, but striking slogan was – 'The Best Navy In The World.'

'. . . I don't know what effect it'll have on recruiting,' said the Recruiting Officer for London and the Home Counties, 'but I do happen to know that our local chemist has sold out of black eyepatches . . .'

'Oh the devil take it all!' The Bodger slammed down the telephone, seized his hat, ran round the corner to The Vaults and sank against the bar where the first person he met was Geoff Pinner.

'*Cap'n!* Matie, I just seen some of your new space! Stupendous!'

'Glad you think so,' said The Bodger, clutching his glass to his chest as though it were a lifebelt. 'Now if you don't mind, I'm going to drink down this glass of whisky very quickly and then I'm going to have another and when that's gone maybe I'll talk about my new space.'

'. . . That traffic scene! Fantabulous! You're in the wrong trade, matie!'

'So it would appear,' said The Bodger.

Geoffrey Pinner was not in the least disconcerted by The Bodger's tale of disaster.

'You got to take the rough with the smooth,' he said. 'Sometimes it comes off. Then again it might not. People are funny, like I told you. Mebbe you ought to be a bit more crafty. Use a bit more psychology. Make it subliminal, like.'

'Subliminal? What's subliminal?'

'You never heard of subliminal advertising? Mebbe I ought not to tell you . . .'

'Why not?'

'I'm not sure it's ethical. To hell with *that*, but I'm not

46

even sure it's legal. Subliminal advertising means you sell a thing to the public without them knowing you're doing it. See what I mean?'

'No.'

'Supposing you have a film. Just an ordinary movie, like a million others, right? Then you cut out a couple of frames of the film and cut in your ad. Just one or two frames at a time. Buy British Beer, say. O.K? The words "Buy British Beer" flash on and off the screen so quick the audience don't even know they've seen it. But their *minds* have seen it! All of a sudden without knowing why, they all feel like a glass of beer. And they can't wait until they get one. See what you've done? You've suggested something to them without them even knowing you've done it!'

'But that's *diabolical!*' The Bodger was horrified.

Geoffrey Pinner smirked. 'It's clever, I grant you.'

'It's like brain-washing!'

'It's very similar, I admit. But it works. It works so damned well we aren't allowed to use it yet.'

'I should think not!'

But in spite of the scruples he had expressed to Geoffrey Pinner, The Bodger could not help turning the idea of subliminal advertising over in his mind. The more The Bodger thought of it, the less unscrupulous and the more attractive it appeared. The idea was simple, unobtrusive and, according to the egregious Mr Pinner, damnably effective. It would surely be worth a try.

The Bodger consulted Pat FitzBeetle, the producer of the Ministry Film Unit, and learned that it was an easy matter to prepare suitable frames and splice them into an existing film. It only remained for The Bodger to find a suitable cinema and this he discovered fifty yards from The Vaults, in the same street.

47

It was a small cinema catering for a limited but devoted clientele. The three films on show when The Bodger came to a meditative halt outside the theatre were *Teenage Stripper*, *Stripper From Outer Space*, and a musical feature entitled *My Bare Lady!* The Bodger pondered for a while and went in.

The cinema manager was an oily man of obviously Levantine origin who, almost as a matter of routine, elicited from The Bodger the assurance that he was over sixteen before proceeding any further. Having further reassured himself that The Bodger was not a policeman, he agreed to give The Bodger's slides a trial showing.

'But no funny business with these slides,' he warned.

'How could there be any funny business,' said The Bodger. 'After all, I'm only plugging the Navy.'

'I have to be careful.' (The Bodger realised that 'slide' had been an unfortunate choice of word.) 'You get some funny characters in this business.'

The Bodger selected the spots for his special frames with care. He arranged for them to be shown during the first film when the heroine was awkwardly and inexpertly auditioning for her first engagement at a striptease club; in the second film when a pale-green artiste from Venus was so charming the assembled world heads of Earth, Mars, Venus and Saturn that an interplanetary war was averted; and during the third feature at a point when twenty-four assorted ladies were disrobing in concert to the strains of *Die Fledermaus*. As he took his seat for the first trial performance The Bodger was pleased to note that the house was full.

Teenage Stripper was described outside the theatre as 'A Heart-Searing Exposé of the Racket in Young Flesh! The Film Every Mother Should See!' and The Bodger became so absorbed in the story that it was not until the entire row

48

in front of him sprang up as one man and bolted for the theatre exit that The Bodger remembered the original purpose of his visit. The first row was quickly followed by another, and by another. The theatre began to empty before The Bodger's astounded eyes.

The Bodger was awed by the success of his subterfuge. This was audience reaction on a scale undreamed-of by the most optimistic public relations man. It seemed that the whole audience were now possessed with the single idea of joining the Navy. The Bodger's conscience smote him as he watched them, male and female, young and old, fighting amongst themselves to be first.

'There's no need to hurry, sir,' he said to a white-haired old man who was endeavouring to trample upon the woman in front of him. 'There's an age limit.'

The old man turned unseeing fanatical eyes upon The Bodger and resumed his struggle to leave the theatre.

By now seriously perturbed by the trick he had played upon a helpless and unsuspecting public, The Bodger hurried into the foyer and found it deserted. The ticket office was empty. The girl who should have been inside it had gone, presumably to join the Wrens. The manager himself was nowhere to be seen. The man had thrown up his job, his prospects, probably his wife and family, to run away to sea.

Determined somehow to put right the wrong he had done, The Bodger ran into the street and almost into the arms of the distracted manager.

'Just got out of there in time,' the manager said.

The Bodger turned round and it was with a sense of genuine relief that he saw the smoke billowing from the roof and realised that the cinema was on fire.

4

The morning after the full extent of the fiasco of The Bodger's venture into high-powered public relations was revealed, The Bodger sat gloomily at his desk, chin on his hands, staring into space. George Dewberry stood by the bookcase, gazing dejectedly at the wall.

'Let's face it, George,' said The Bodger. 'The Navy just doesn't respond to normal methods. I'm beginning to understand now just what was griping Jimmy. We need something really extraordinary to get us out of the rut. Something with naval connections but which the ordinary Joe in the street will be interested in.'

'If it's going to interest the ordinary Joe in the street, sir, it'll have to be about football pools or horse racing.'

'Horse racing,' said The Bodger meditatively. 'Your horse is a racehorse, George.'

'Yes, sir. It hasn't shown much form yet, but it's by the same sire as La Petite so it ought to turn out all right eventually.'

'What was that name?'

'La Petite.'

'What's so special about La Petite?'

'La Petite, sir!' George Dewberry seemed staggered by The Bodger's innocence. 'She's the best two-year-old of the season sir! She's the punter's friend. Unbeaten in five races so far this year. People are saying she's the best racing filly since Pretty Polly. She was backed down to 100–30 *on* in the Cheveley Park Stakes yesterday and it was like picking up

50

money in the street! She won by ten lengths and according to the newspapers she was never off the bit the whole way. The jockey still had a double handful at the line!'

The Bodger shook his head. 'George, I hear you but I don't understand you. This is a new language to me.'

The Bodger's ignorance of the Sport of Kings, unusual in a serving naval officer, was nevertheless excusable because his sub-lieutenants' courses (the traditional time for a young officer's instruction in all matters concerning the Turf) had taken place during the war when there had been only a small amount of zoned racing. Having been denied his proper opportunities early in life The Bodger had never subsequently shown any interest in the sport and although he had some slight knowledge of the principles of placing bets he was still as ignorant as a Hottentot of flat-racing in general. Nevertheless, George Dewberry had unwittingly sown a tiny seed. The ghost of an idea, as yet intangible and insubstantial, was slowly taking shape in The Bodger's mind.

'Did you say this horse of yours was entered for the Derby, George?'

'Yes sir, as far as I know. I'll have to check with the trainer, but I do know that all my aunt's horses were always entered for all the Classics and the trainer always had a terrible job to get her to scratch them.'

'Tell me, can we go down and see it?'

'Why yes, sir.' George Dewberry was startled by The Bodger's sudden interest. 'It's stabled down near Newbury, which is only a couple of hours by car. If you hold on a minute, sir, I'll give the trainer a ring.'

When George Dewberry had gone, The Bodger sat pensively in his chair. The germ of his idea was shooting out roots. Now, it had reached the open and was beginning to flourish. A grey colt named Battlewagon, owned perhaps by a syndicate from the Naval Public Relations Department, running in the Derby! *There* would be a story for the newspapers! And if it *won!* The Bodger pictured the scene in his mind's eye: a lovely day at Epsom, his wife Julia leading in the Derby winner, the cheering crowds, the hats sailing into the air, the beaming jockey with his goggles pushed up over his cap, the horse lathered in sweat after running the fastest – that was a point! How long *was* the Derby course? The Bodger had no idea whether it was one mile, two miles or five miles. It might even be ten miles, for all he knew.

'I've rung the trainer, sir . . .'

The Bodger roused himself from his glorious day-dreams.

'. . . He says the horse *is* entered for the Derby, though he can't think why. A selling plate would be nearer his mark. He says he's off to Pontefract tomorrow and he's busy the rest of the week but if we'd like to come down this afternoon, he'll be happy to see us and show us the horse.'

'That's fine. I'll drive you down after lunch. By the way George, how long is the Derby course?'

'One and a half miles, sir.'

'I thought so. Gwladys,' The Bodger said into the Squawk Box. 'I'm going out to lunch now and I won't be back afterwards. I'm going to see a man about a horse.'

'Very good, sir,' said Gwladys distantly.

*   *   *

The Bodger's car was a dignified maroon Alvis and he drove it with the confidence of a Roman general driving his chariot through a triumph.

'Fussy little pressed out *bug!*' he said, as he intimidated with a glare a small family saloon which attempted to draw out in front of him. 'What do you intend to do with this horse, George?'

'I haven't thought about it yet. I suppose I ought to sell it but I have a kind of hankering to run it.'

'And I have a strange sort of hankering to join you,' said The Bodger.

'I'm willing sir, if you'd like to halve the expenses with me.'

'It'll be quite something to have a horse running in the Derby!'

'Oh, I don't think this horse will ever run in the Derby. From what the trainer says, I gather it's not much good.'

'In spite of being a grandson of Airborne out of a Hyperion mare?'

George Dewberry laughed. 'In *spite* of that, sir. You can pay ten thousand guineas for a horse and never win a race with him. You can have a horse with Derby and Oaks winners all over its pedigree and yet for some reason or other it won't even stand training. It's a hell of a chancy business.'

'I'm beginning to see that. Do you know where these stables are, George?'

'Yes, sir. We used to go down quite a lot three years ago when my aunt thought she had a Derby winner.'

'What happened then?'

'Broke a fetlock and had to be destroyed.'

'Oh dear.'

Directed by George Dewberry, The Bodger drove through Newbury and turned off the main road a few miles west of the town. At once they came upon signs of one of the main industries of the area. Beyond the trees by the road a line of white painted rails enclosed a stretch of churned turf. A practice starting-gate stood at the far end. They passed a notice 'Danger: Racehorses Crossing' and just beyond it they saw a Land Rover parked by the roadside.

'I think that's his Land Rover, sir.'

There were two men standing in the middle of the gallop, peering at the turf like cricketers inspecting the pitch. One of them was wearing a dark raincoat and a cloth cap; the other was a slightly-built, bareheaded man with hair as red as Swinburne's and a pale delicate face as though he had just stepped out of a Pre-Raphaelite painting.

'That's Commander Terry-Neames, sir, the trainer.'

The Bodger stopped the car and got out. 'I certainly recognise that name,' he said, 'and I think I recognise that face.'

As they came nearer, the red-haired man turned and saw them.

'Wotcher George!' Then he noticed The Bodger. '*Bodger!*'

'*Poggles*, you old wineskin!'

Plainly, The Bodger and George Dewberry's late aunt's trainer were no strangers; indeed they were old friends and drinking partners.

'You thinking of becoming a racehorse owner, Bodger? Last time I saw you you were teaching cadets how to be officers and gentlemen!'

'What are *you* doing as a racehorse *trainer*, Poggles? Last time I saw you you were poking "*Rowbottom*" round the ocean.'

Poggles laughed. 'It's good to see you again anyway, Bodger.'

'It's good to see you too, Poggles. But seriously, when did all this happen?'

'It's a long story,' said Poggles. 'My father started this stable when he left the Army but he died just about the time I got my golden bowler from the Navy. So I took it over.'

'How are you doing?'

Poggles shrugged. 'Not bad. Can't complain. At least I'm full up. I'm not exactly desperate for business now. It was a bit sticky to start with, though. You've come to look at that grey, haven't you?'

'Battlewagon,' said The Bodger, with a touch of pride.

'Big grey stiff.' Poggles nodded to the man in the raincoat. 'Right Ben, see you tomorrow.'

Ben touched his cap. 'Right, Guv'nor.'

'Let's go up to the office and talk about this,' Poggles said to The Bodger.

'Who's Ben?' George Dewberry asked.

'He looks after the gallops.'

'You have a special bloke to look after the gallops?' said The Bodger.

'Two, actually.'

'Blimey,' said The Bodger.

Poggles grinned as he climbed into his Land Rover. 'You pay them. Or rather the owners, collectively, do.'

The training stables were in the form of a square, with the south side removed. Two of the three remaining sides contained the loose boxes and the third the tack rooms, feeding barn, store rooms and Poggles' office. The boxes were built of brick with boarded and slated roofs, the doors and window frames were freshly tar-varnished and the steel door straps were shining. The Bodger was impressed by the cleanliness and tidiness of the place. The yard itself was so clean it looked as if it had been polished. Beyond the stables The Bodger could see another paddock which led up to the gallops and a sprawling house in a small orchard which was presumably Poggles' home.

'What do you think of it, Bodger?'

'I must say I'm very impressed. It's a lot more organised than I expected. It's . . . what's the word I'm looking for? It's like an industry.'

'It *is* an industry,' said Poggles, 'and a very highly specialised one at that.'

A motor horse box was drawn up in the yard. Poggles' head lad and one of the stable lads were attempting to lead a coal-black filly up the ramp. The filly was nervous and was skittering away every time they led her towards the horse box. The stable lad was hanging desperately to the bridle, while the head lad swore enthusiastically.

'Where's that horse going?'

'She's a filly. Little Black Bikini is her name. She's running at Pontefract tomorrow and she's got a very good chance, if you care to have something on her. We're running her in blinkers, which means she's expected.'

'*Expectant!*' exclaimed The Bodger. 'You don't mean you're running her when she's pregnant!'

'*Expected*, not expectant!' Poggles laughed out loud, so that the filly bucked frantically. 'I mean she's fancied tomorrow. We don't normally run mares when they're in foal, though it has been done. You'd be surprised what they can do. My wife once got third prize at a show and her mare foaled three weeks later. Normally the fact that a filly is in season is enough to stop her running. Amiss, we call it. A few fillies actually run better when they're amiss but the vast majority run well below form. This little girl is dead lazy so we give her blinkers to keep her mind on her work. If we just want to give her a try-out, without much thought of winning, we run her without blinkers. That's worth remembering, if you're interested.'

The head lad had succeeded in cajoling Little Black Bikini on to the ramp. There she stuck adamantly.

'Bikini doesn't like my voice,' Poggles said. 'It reminds her of hard work. Just watch.'

Poggles walked quietly towards the filly. The head lad saw him coming and guessed his purpose.

'Ah, don't do that, Guv'nor,' he pleaded. 'We almost got her in.'

'Steady, gel,' Poggles said, in a low voice.

The effect was dramatic. Little Black Bikini reared and plunged as though prodded with a red-hot poker and then, wishing to escape from the voice of her taskmaster, trotted up the ramp and into the horsebox. The head lad looked at Poggles reproachfully.

Poggles, grinning shamefacedly, came back to The Bodger. 'I shouldn't have done that,' he said.

'It did the trick,' The Bodger pointed out.

'I know, but she might have injured herself. A racehorse's legs are made of fine porcelain, you know. I sometimes think you can send one of these horses lame just by looking hard at its fetlocks. Well, let's go into the office and have a glass of whisky and talk about Battlewagon. I suppose you'll be wanting me to find a buyer, George . . .'

The Bodger and George Dewberry exchanged glances.

'Well, not exactly,' George Dewberry mumbled.

Poggles' office was the heart of the stable. From there he administered the daily routine of the establishment, deciding which horses should exercise and how fast, which horses should be rested, and how much food they all should be given to eat. There he interviewed stable lads who had been caught smoking in stables or who had turned out their horses looking slovenly for exercise. There, he battled with his finances, juggling bills for feed, bills for hay, blacksmith's bills, saddler's bills, and the veterinary surgeon's fees. Poggles spent hours in his office 'doing his homework' – studying the

Racing Calendar, the *Stud Book*, *Raceform* and letters from his owners demanding that their horses run at Royal Ascot, in a never-ending attempt to place his horses in races where they had a chance of winning. In his office Poggles composed those tactful letters which took up so much of his time – to one owner breaking the news that his colt had begun to make what sounded suspiciously like a noise, to another owner suggesting that her horse was badly weighted for the Ascot Stakes but there was another promising race at Yarmouth a week later, and to a third owner explaining that his filly's failure to be placed on Saturday was not due, as he had insinuated, to an inherent defect in her training schedule but was the result of the filly's own inexplicable inability to run faster than the other fillies in the race.

None of this The Bodger appreciated as he looked round the office. He saw a tiny room full of assorted saddlery, photographs of racehorses in various attitudes of extended motion, a paraffin stove and a large antique desk heaped with papers, volumes of the *Stud Book*, old copies of *Ruff's* and the *Racing Calendar* and, on top of the desk, a superb metal model of a racehorse. It was an upstanding colt with strong sloping shoulders, a deep chest, straight hindlegs and a short but intelligent head.

'What horse is that?'

'Isinglass, by Isonomy out of Deadlock. One of the greatest racehorses ever. Won the Two Thousand Guineas, the Derby and the Leger.'

'Did your old man train it or something?'

'Have a heart, Bodger! The animal was foaled in 1890! My father bought that model in Port Said during the First World War. He was wandering along some bazaar or other and suddenly there was this horse. He looked at the label on it and dammit it was Isinglass! The colour's not quite right. Isinglass was a bay, but otherwise it's a good likeness. My old man could remember my grandfather talking about Isinglass. The horse was a walking miracle. Apart from the three Classics he also won the Middle Park Stakes, the New Stakes at Ascot, the Princess of Wales Stakes, the Jockey Club Stakes, the Eclipse Stakes and the Ascot Gold Cup. You name it, Isinglass won it. But that's not the best part about my friend Isinglass . . .'

Poggles took a tooth glass from a shelf and placed it under the horse. There was a gurgling sound and the horse squirted a measure of whisky, *per via naturalis*, into the glass.

'It's some sort of trick mechanism in the base,' Poggles explained. 'If you leave the glass there, he'll go on gurgling and peeing until the glass is full. He holds two bottles,' Poggles added, proudly.

George Dewberry's admiration of the model had been increased tenfold by the demonstration. 'That's bloody marvellous!' he said. 'How do you fill him?'

'Unscrew his head and pour the stuff in.'

'Bloody marvellous!'

When Isinglass had filled three glasses, Poggles said: 'Cheers, Bodger. Here's to the old *Rowbottom*, bless her rusty sides. Talking of the Classics, we've never saddled a Classic winner from here. But we keep hoping. My father once saddled the second favourite for the Derby but he didn't finish anywhere.'

'How would you like another go at the Derby next year?' The Bodger said, keeping his voice level.

'Using what for a horse?'

'Battlewagon.'

Poggles set his glass firmly down on his desk. 'Bodger, I know you're an old friend of mine,' he said, painfully, 'but

I don't think that's at all amusing. This stable here may seem rather comical to you, an ex-naval officer amusing himself training racehorses . . .'

'Poggles, I didn't for a minute . . .'

'. . . I can assure you I *do* run a business here and I *do* make money at it. Not much, but some.'

'Poggles, I hadn't any intention of making funny remarks about your business . . .'

'Suggesting Battlewagon for the Derby *is* a funny remark. Funny peculiar.'

'He's a grandson of Airborne out of a Hyperion mare,' said The Bodger.

'Oh, the *breeding's* all right, I'll give you that. It could be better, mind you, but . . . George, you're keeping very quiet, what d'you think about this? After all, it's your horse.'

George Dewberry had been lost in contemplation of his whisky. He had vaguely guessed at what was passing through The Bodger's mind on the journey down in the car but he had given it no serious thought. Nobody would ever unravel the impulses which moved George Dewberry at that critical moment, whether it was the whisky, or the dazzling revelation of Isinglass's internal resources, or whether it was simply an impish spirit of pure bravado, but he came to an inspired decision.

'I would like Battlewagon to run in the Derby,' he said firmly.

'*George!* Hell's teeth, I had this trouble with your aunt! It must run in the family!' Poggles took a deep breath. 'It seems I'd better educate you fellows about horse racing.'

Poggles paused while Isinglass refilled his glass.

'The Derby Stakes,' said Poggles heavily, 'is a race for three-year-old entire colts and fillies, run over one mile and a half at Epsom in the summer each year, the colts to carry nine stone and the fillies to carry eight stone nine pounds.

It costs two hundred quid in forfeits to run a horse in the Derby and there are 519 subscriptions for next year's race. There's also ten thousand sovereigns added to the stake money and the value to the winner nowadays runs out at about thirty thousand quid or more. That's the official description of the race and how much you can win. But the Derby isn't like other races. The Derby's a dream. It's an ideal. It's almost a mirage. People have poured *thousands* into the Turf and died without leading in a Derby winner.'

'What went wrong?' The Bodger said.

'I don't know. If I did I wouldn't be here. I would be breeding Derby winners as a business and be worth several million by now. I can only tell you what *won't* win the Derby. Money won't do it. Some fabulously expensive colts have run nowhere in the Derby, yet Hard Ridden cost two hundred and eighty-three pounds ten shillings as a yearling and Charlie Smirke brought him home by *five* lengths. *Breeding* won't do it. You've got to have it, but it's not enough by itself. You'd think that all you had to do was put the sire of the winner to the same dam again and get another Derby winner. If that were so, a dozen horses would dead-heat for the Derby next year. But it isn't so. If you try the same combination again you *may* get two Derby winners, Persimmon and Diamond Jubilee were both full brothers, by St Simon out of Perdita the Second, but that's *very* unusual. If you get three horses from the same sire and dam you're more likely to get one good horse, if you're lucky, one reasonable horse, and one thoroughly useless hunk of horse-flesh. Our old friend Isinglass is a good example of what normally happens. He won £57,455 in prize money, including the Derby, and you can imagine how much that was worth in the 1890's. Yet his full brother Islington won only £980 during his career. Physical conformation won't win the Derby either. Dozens of perfectly-made colts have carried their backers' money down the drain with them but Gladiateur, who won in 1865, suffered from chronic fetlock trouble and was almost permanently lame. His dam Miss Gladiator was such a crock she never raced at all! You'd think experience of the racecourse would be essential for a horse to win the Derby but Middleton and Amato both won the Derby. In both cases it was the *only* race of their career!' Poggles shook his head in wonder. 'There's no common factor for Derby winners. All sorts of horses have won it. Running Rein won it in 1844 and he was a four-year-old ringer . . .'

'What's a ringer?' asked The Bodger.

'A fake. His real name was Maccabeus. Some crafty customer slipped him in with the yearlings while he was a two-year-old so he was really a four-year-old when he won the Derby. The Stewards of the Jockey Club found out about it afterwards and gave the race to Orlando, who was second. But that didn't bring all the lost money back.'

'That was a pretty crooked trick,' said The Bodger.

'We've got some hard cases in racing. Always have had.'

'To get back to the Derby, Poggles, you were saying you don't know what makes a Derby winner.'

'I seem to have been going on about this rather a long time . . .'

'Don't worry about that. It's all news to me.'

'To sum up then. To win the Derby you've got to have a horse bred from the top class. Before he gets to the course he mustn't damage his legs, sprain his back, break a blood vessel, get nobbled or any of the thousand things that can happen to a horse in training. Once he gets to the course he mustn't be worried by about thirty other frantic horses all milling round him at the start and he mustn't be put off by all the shouting and tumult. Once he gets going he must stay a mile and a half, he must go down Tattenham Hill well, come round Tattenham Corner like a trolley and he must quicken up the last hill. He must have a jockey who can ride a Derby winner, who doesn't get himself trapped on the rails, who doesn't make his move too early or too late, who isn't frightened of winning the Derby and who can win it without getting disqualified afterwards. One last thing . . .' Poggles paused significantly. '. . . your horse must be born in a year when there isn't *another* horse who can do all the things I've mentioned better than he can! You give me all that and I can promise you you'll be leading in a Derby winner next year. Now what d'you say? Do you still want him to run?'

'Yes!' said George Dewberry, without hesitation.

'Well *said*, George!' cried The Bodger. 'I'm with you!'

Poggles pursed his lips grimly. 'I think we'd better go down and take a look at our Derby winner. He's down in the bottom paddock.'

Poggles led the way outside and they all climbed into the Land Rover. Poggles remained forbiddingly silent while they bumped down a lane to the bottom paddock and neither The Bodger nor George Dewberry felt that polite conversation was called for.

Poggles stopped the Land Rover abruptly.

'There,' he said.

The Bodger looked over a gate and saw a grey animal standing in the distance.

'Name of a name,' he said. 'I see what you mean, Poggles. He doesn't look big enough to give children rides at the seaside.'

'*What?*' Poggles arched himself in his seat and stared over the gate. Then he fell across the steering wheel, laughing like a dervish.

'Bodger,' he said, 'you'll be the death of me! That's Bill, the donkey we put in there to keep Battlewagon company! Not big enough to give children rides at the seaside! *Cor!*'

'I'm sorry I'm a bit clueless about all this,' said The Bodger ruefully, as he dismounted from the Land Rover.

'That's all right, Bodger. You do me good. Most of my owners come down here and tell *me* what to do. It's a change to meet a completely fresh outlook. There's your horse, down at the end.'

Battlewagon had already observed their arrival and was ambling slowly towards them; clearly, economy of movement was his motto in life. He was a rangy colt, still a trifle on the leg, with heavy shoulders, a proud head and liquid, kindly eyes. Battlewagon stopped a few yards away and pricked his ears, gazing directly at The Bodger, as though appraising The Bodger's chances in the Derby.

'What do you think of him?'

'He's a beautiful animal,' said The Bodger.

Poggles grunted. 'He'll make some milkman a good friend some day,' he said caustically.

'What's his next race?' George Dewberry asked.

'I don't think he's got one. I can't remember offhand but knowing your late aunt, with all due respect, George, I expect he's entered for something exotic like the Middle Park Stakes. Unless I've remembered to scratch him.'

'Can't he run in that?' said The Bodger.

Poggles had by now accustomed himself to the fact that he and The Bodger no longer spoke the same language. 'The Middle Park Stakes is a race for the top two-year-olds of the season,' he explained patiently.

'Well, can't he run in it? At least it'll tell us what he's like.'

'I can tell you now what he's like. Bloody useless.'

Battlewagon ducked and shook his head so that his mane rippled, and blew heavily through his nostrils. Then he suddenly raised his head and looked straight at The Bodger. The look went to The Bodger's heart. It said, more plainly than words, 'If you believe *that*, Buster, you'll believe anything!'

'. . . We ran him in a race at Hurst Park at the beginning of the season,' Poggles was saying. 'He went off with a bang, stayed four furlongs and ran on very gamely to finish last. His next outing was at Newmarket in late April. Again he ran like a champion, enjoyed every minute of it and finished a very competent last. Then we tried him here at Newbury. He huffed and he puffed and he threw his jockey off as the tapes went up. Even then, without carrying a jockey, he still finished last.'

Battlewagon had turned his head away while Poggles was speaking and was now staring at a point beyond the trees at the end of the paddock.

'What's he doing now?' said George Dewberry.

'God knows. Ask him. He does that occasionally. He stands there looking out to sea for half an hour at a time. His grandsire Hyperion used to do it and so did his great-great grandsire Bayardo. I just let him get on with it.'

'He's probably thinking of the Derby,' The Bodger said mischievously.

'Look here, Bodger,' said Poggles in exasperation. 'Let's settle this argument once and for all. Would you like me to arrange a special trial for Battlewagon? We'll jump him off with a couple of other decent horses so that you can see for yourself.'

'That sounds like an excellent idea, Poggles.'

'I'm busy the rest of this week, but how about Sunday?'

'I think I can manage that.'

'You be here ten o'clock next Sunday morning and we'll jump Battlewagon off properly. Bring Julia and stay afterwards for lunch. How about that?'

'We'll be there,' The Bodger promised.

5

'Hear you've got yourself a racehorse, sir,' the hall porter said to The Bodger when he arrived at the Ministry the next morning.

'That's right.'

'Any good, sir?'

'It's a grandson of Airborne out of a Hyperion mare,' said The Bodger casually, and was gratified to see that the hall porter looked impressed.

'Thought you said you wasn't a racing man, sir?'

'Ah well, I didn't want to advertise it.'

'I *quite* agree, sir. You got to be discreet about these matters.' The hall porter pulled out his copy of *Sporting Life*. 'Got anything on for today, sir?'

The Bodger was about to disclaim any special knowledge of the runners or the riders when his eye caught the name Pontefract.

'Yes, as a matter of fact I have. Let me have a look. There you are. Three-thirty. Little Black Bikini. They're running her in blinkers today, you know.'

'Are they, sir? Now, that's *very* interesting. I wondered why she was going all that way, sir. I said to myself Terry-Neames don't send a filly all the way up to Pontefract just to meet some of her relations. Are you going to have something on her, sir?'

'Yes, put me on a fiver to win, will you?' said The Bodger, in a voice which he was amazed to hear was his own.

The hall porter's eyebrows shot upwards. 'Like *that* is it, sir?'

'Yes,' said The Bodger, and marched jauntily off towards his office as though he confidently expected to find the entire Jockey Club waiting inside.

'You must be *mad*, Bodger,' he said to himself. 'Putting a fiver on a horse like that. You haven't even *got* a fiver till the end of the month!'

There were no members of the Jockey Club waiting in The Bodger's office. Instead there was Pat FitzBeetle, the producer of the Ministry Film Unit, who was sitting in The Bodger's chair and apparently going through his drawers.

'And the top of the morning to you, Bodger!' Pat Fitz-Beetle, a Londoner born and bred, affected the speech of a native of Dublin, though normally only first thing in the morning and last thing at night. 'I was just looking for the bottle of something Jimmy used to keep in his bottom drawer.'

'It was empty, so I ditched it,' said The Bodger.

'Sure and that's a pity!'

'What can I do for you, Pat?'

'I wanted to discuss this film unit we're sending down to *Octopus*. We'd better start making the preliminary overtures quite soon.'

'I haven't heard about this one. What's the story?'

'It's all part of Navy Schools Week. We're going to do a documentary. A Day At Sea In A Modern Frigate, or something. We haven't fixed the details yet.'

'Leave it with me a day or two, will you? Just give me a chance to read up some of the background.'

'There's no hurry. We shouldn't have any trouble arranging it. Guess who's the Captain of the good ship *Octopus?*'

'Who?'

'No less a personage than our late Lord High Executioner, Jimmy Forster-Jones. By the way Bodger, I gather you're becoming a patron of the Turf?'

'In a very small way,' The Bodger admitted.

'You should go and see Bert Beattle, our statistician. He's a wizard at picking winners. The Derby is his forte. He cranks up his mighty machine and calculates who's going to win.'

'Is he any good at it?'

'He's given the winner, three races out of five.'

'*Has* he?'

'The horse he picks is normally in the first four at least. He came up with Panaslipper a few years ago. It started at a hundred to one and was only beaten by one and a half lengths.'

'I must go and see this man,' said The Bodger.

Bert Beattle's office was at the end of the corridor, opposite Angus MacBeetle, the Sea Cadet Liaison Officer. The Bodger found Bert Beattle sitting in front of a wide wall of electronic machinery which was in furious operation. Plainly, the mighty machine was racking its brains. Lights were winking on and off. Reels of tape were revolving. Gauge needles were oscillating in simple harmonic motion. Bert Beattle himself was totting up figures on a small pad. He was a friendly little man with china-blue eyes and thin fair hair. The Bodger imagined him as the kind of man whose wife would always be ready to baby-sit or look after the cat and who would himself always be the first to run after a hat which had been blown off by the wind.

'Am I disturbing you?' said The Bodger.

'Not at all, not at all,' said Bert Beattle hospitably. 'I'm just hanging on the slack while Admiralty A.R.C.H.I.E finishes his programme.'

'Who's Admiralty Archie?'

'That,' said Bert Beattle, waving his hand to include the electronic wall and the various black boxes stacked along one side of the office. 'Admiralty Articulated Computing Hierarchy Enumerator.'

'Golly,' said The Bodger. 'What's he working out for you?'

'I'm trying to evaluate a working cycle of refits, dockings, maintenance periods, recommissioning dates and paying-off dates for all the ships in the Navy. We're not having much success at the moment because there are too many ships and they go to sea too often.'

'Well, *that's* an unusual complaint!' said The Bodger. '*I* thought we didn't have enough ships and they didn't go to sea often enough.'

'Not as far as Admiralty Archie is concerned.'

'Why don't you try a smaller selection?' The Bodger suggested. 'Say, half the number. Just to give you a start.'

'And then work out a theoretical hypothesis which can be augmented later to cover more possibilities?'

'I suppose that's what I mean,' said The Bodger doubtfully.

'That's a very good idea. Thank you very much!'

The Bodger glanced down at the scribbled figures on Bert Beattle's pad. 'I see you've been giving Archie a helping hand.'

'Oh no.' Bert Beattle seemed embarrassed. 'I was just working out how much my season ticket costs me.'

'Why don't you let Archie work it out?'

'I daren't. He'd tell me it wasn't worth it and I ought to walk.'

'Is it true you're a wizard at the horses, Bert?'

'I only do the Derby. It takes too long to set Archie up.'

'Have you had any success?'

'I started in 1931. My first winner was April the Fifth. That was long before I had Archie, of course, and the errors were much larger. Now I've got him I've had three winners in the last five races. The longest priced winner I've had was Pearl Diver at 40–1. The shortest was Crepello at 6–4. Of course I didn't need Archie to work that one out.'

'How do you do it?'

'It would take too long to explain properly . . .'

'Briefly, then.'

'Briefly, I prepare what I call the "profile" of the ideal Derby winner. I include everything I can think of, breeding, conformation, stamina, past form and so on. Then there's special factors, the jockey, the trainer, the going, the weather, even the ante-post betting. I've got thirty-seven separate criteria for judging a Derby winner. When I've got my master profile I feed it into Archie and as he's got a kind of memory he holds it while I prepare individual profiles of every horse left in the race. I feed the individual profiles into Archie and he evaluates and compares them against the master profile and produces four horses which come nearest to the master profile. I put those four horses back into Archie and he compares them and calculates a mean profile for that year's Derby. Finally, Archie compares the four initial selections against the mean for that year's Derby and the one that comes nearest is my selection for the Derby.'

'Good God,' said The Bodger.

'Sometimes Archie comes up with information I can't use. One of the best Derby profiles I ever saw was Alcide, who never ran. He injured himself just before the race. Archie isn't infallible by a long way. There are always factors which are difficult to assess. French and Irish form is always hard to judge, particularly Irish. Then again a horse may travel to the course badly and I don't know anything about that until the race is over. But by and large Archie produces a good each-way bet at least.'

'I think it's amazing,' said The Bodger sincerely. Making

a mental note to pay a call on Bert Beattle just before the Derby, The Bodger reached his own office and found the telephone ringing.

'Jim Sewter here, Amalgamated Press Bureau . . .'

'Oh yes, I remember you,' said The Bodger, coldly.

'Morning, Bodger! All parts taking an even strain?'

'What can I do for you?'

'We've had a report that HMS *Octopus* has had a fire on board. Any comment?'

'This is news to me . . .'

'That's our business, boy!'

'Just leave it with me will you, Jim? I'll ring you back.'

'O.K. Bodger. How's it going, by the way?'

'Splendid.'

'Don't believe you. See you.'

Before The Bodger had had a chance to collect his thoughts, his telephone rang again.

'Stephen Ropehead here, Naval Correspondent of the *Daily Disaster*. One of our men has just phoned a story that HMS *Octopus*'s boiler rooms have been burnt out . . .'

'Just leave this one with me, will you? I'll ring you back as soon as I can.'

'Right.'

The next call asked whether it was true that HMS *Octopus* was burning fiercely from end to end; the fourth call asked for confirmation of the story that firemen had fought all night without success to save HMS *Octopus* from becoming a burnt-out hulk. After that, The Bodger kept his thumb firmly on the telephone, lifted it off quickly and asked the exchange to get him HMS *Octopus*. After a series of atmospheric effects which suggested that some unskilled hand was dismantling a runaway tram, The Bodger was connected to the inevitably moronic Quartermaster.

'HMS *Octopus* 'ere.'

'This is Commander Badger, Naval Public Relations Department ...'

'Eh?'

'This is Commander Badger speaking ...'

'*Eh?*'

'*Commander Badger!*' bellowed The Bodger.

'Commander 'Oo?'

'Can I speak to the *Captain?*'

'The Captain. 'Oo's speaking?'

'Just get the *Captain!*'

The telephone receiver was dropped with a thump which passed right through The Bodger's eardrums. The Bodger could hear a lengthy argument, shouts, a silence, further argument and then the voice of the mongolian Quartermaster once more.

'The Captain says if that's the newspapers again tell them to take a running —— at a rolling doughnut.'

'It's Commander *Badger!*' pleaded The Bodger.

'Give me that! Hello!' said Jimmy Forster-Jones brusquely.

'Good morning Jimmy, it's The Bodger ...'

'Hello Bodger, what d'you want?' snapped Jimmy Forster-Jones.

'Jimmy, everyone's asking me about a fire ...'

'It was a small fire in the electrical spare gear store,' Jimmy recited, in a voice which made it clear that he had already told the story many times. 'There was no damage and there were no casualties. That what you want to know?'

'You might have told me first, Jimmy,' said The Bodger reproachfully. 'You of all people ought to know ...'

'Why should I tell you? Is that all you wanted to talk to me about?'

The Bodger realised that it was hardly an auspicious

moment to broach the subject of the film unit but now that he had Jimmy actually on the line he felt bound to seize the opportunity; he dared not risk the cretinous Quartermaster at some time in the future.

'Jimmy, we'd like to bring a film unit down to *Octopus* . . .'

'What for?'

'We want to do a documentary . . .'

'Why?'

'It's for Navy Schools Week . . .'

'Blast Navy Schools Week!'

'But Jimmy!' cried The Bodger desperately. 'This is what you were telling me about! Public relations and all that . . .'

'Blast public relations. I've got a ship to run here, not a three-ring circus! I haven't got time to mess about with film units! Good-bye!'

Stricken by the astonishing metamorphosis which had overtaken his old friend, The Bodger constructed a careful account of the accident to HMS *Octopus* and released it to the press. That done, he composed himself to wait patiently for the evening papers. If his last brush with the press was any criterion, the evening's headlines would once again bring Admiral Gilpin down upon him like Sennacherib. The Bodger could visualise the banners, the newsboys shouting 'Fire in Frigate', 'Warship Inferno', 'Sabotage Suspected?', and 'Hot as Hell in there,' says A.B.

Yet, strangely, there was no visitation from that bird of ill-omen, the Tatler and Bystander. The Admiral's line on the Squawk Box remained silent. The Bodger sat drumming his fingers on his desk in anxiety. He looked about him for some means of distraction. He remembered that Jimmy had said that George de Beetle, who wrote Admiralty Fleet Orders, was worth calling on. Admiralty Fleet Orders, known generally by their abbreviated title of AFOs, were published weekly for the guidance of the Fleet. They provided detailed information and instructions on every part of naval life; there was no facet of the Navy which was not fully covered in AFOs and The Bodger had always imagined that they were produced by a whole department of civil servants working at full pressure in a building at least the size of the Ministry of Political Warfare itself. The idea that they were all the work of one man, in one office, The Bodger found scarcely credible.

When The Bodger saw George de Beetle's office his first thought was that he had inadvertently strayed into some form of museum or theatre props room. The room was a jumble of clothes, hats, boxes, piles of books and heaps of unidentifiable junk. A range of false beards, from a luxuriant white Shavian to a ginger beatnik fringe, hung on a peg. On a small table next to a tape-recorder were a sombrero, a pair of chukker boots, an ear-trumpet and a plaster model of a lobster. A glass tank containing several barnacles stood on the window-sill and on the wall, above a row of assorted coats, shawls and a matador's fighting cape, hung two pictures, one of a small dog of indeterminate breed and the other of a hard-faced beefy-armed woman who stared at The Bodger with an expression of contempt. The centre of the room was dominated by a gleaming chrome and plastic cabinet studded with levers and buttons, like a miniature Martian cinema organ. Seated on a stool in front of the machine was a tiny wisp of a man, completely bald, wearing a faded grey overall. He was sitting motionless, apparently gazing at a white stetson on the wall.

'Mr de Beetle?' The Bodger said tentatively.

The little man swung round on his stool and faced The Bodger.

'You're the new Assistant Director,' he said, getting off

his stool to shake hands. 'How very kind of you to call. I'm very pleased to meet you, sir.'

'I just thought I'd take a walk round and start meeting everybody in the department,' The Bodger said. 'I'm told you write *all* the AFOs?'

George de Beetle cast his eyes down. 'That's true,' he admitted.

'How on earth do you do it, all by yourself?'

George de Beetle waved a vague hand round his office. 'I need atmosphere,' he said. 'So I have my props. That's Beethoven's ear-trumpet on the table. I sometimes use the Heiligenstadt Testament technique, you know. Those barnacles in the tank are the lineal descendants of Charles Darwin's. The "Evolution" approach is sometimes very useful. The lobster is a facsimile of Gérard de Nerval's. That's Molière's cook in the picture there, and Newton's dog Diamond. On the wall there, G. K. Chesterton's cape and Jack London's sleeping bag. The deerstalker is a fake I'm afraid; it's not Holmes's though I did buy it in Baker Street. And of course,' George de Beetle patted the Martian cinema organ affectionately, 'there's always A.L.F.I.E.'

'*Alfie?*'

George de Beetle nodded. 'Admiralty Literary Filing and Indexing Enumerator. It helps me set the mood. Would you like to see how it's done?'

'Very much,' said The Bodger.

'I was just about to do a brief for the Director of Air Training. I think I've got it now.'

George de Beetle took a purple-bordered toga from a hook behind the door and threw it round his shoulders. Then he placed an olive sprig on his temples and pressed A.L.F.I.E Button 'MACAULAY'.

At once, the tumultuous chords of the opening of the last

movement of Beethoven's Choral Symphony reverberated round the office. The room darkened. George de Beetle's features assumed an Homeric cast. His eyes flashed the fire which once enslaved Prometheus. Darkness fell from the office air. The walls shook to the immortal clangour of gods at war, unearthly lightning flickered on the spectral bronze helmets of the Heavenly Twins by the window and the dint of Black Auster's hooves splintered the office floorboards.

'. . . A case has recently occurred . . .' George de Beetle was thundering, in iambics, 'of two pilots attempting to enter the same cockpit simultaneously . . .'

The room had returned to its original creative silence and George de Beetle was back in his grey overall again before The Bodger could properly recollect himself. The Bodger was still roaming the plains of Tusculum and striking cascades of sparks from the plumed helmet of Prince Mamilius with his inspired sword. 'Holy mother of all the crocodiles!' he breathed, at last. 'That was *unbelievable!*'

George de Beetle shrugged. 'That's nothing,' he said modestly. 'You should see me when I get on to Victualling Stores.'

George de Beetle pressed A.L.F.I.E Button 'MIDDLE EAST' and pouted sensuous, James Elroy Flecker lips. An ornamental grille slid over the window and the silhouettes of interesting Orientals passed to and fro beyond it. A subtle scent of spices pervaded the air. Above the murmuring of water from a fountain and the low groans of a man enduring the bastinado the music of Delius flooded in as though from a garden in paradise while George de Beetle compiled the inventory of goods for the next caravan to take the Golden Road to Samarkand.

'. . . Admiralty pattern carpets, Turkish, 12 ft. by 20 ft., Flag Officers, for the use of . . .'

Again The Bodger took some time to return to normality. His absorption both amused and delighted George de Beetle; it was not often that George de Beetle had such a rewarding audience.

'Try me on Medical Stores,' he said, stringing a mosquito net across the office and putting on a battered pith helmet.

'Used to belong to Rudyard Kipling,' he explained to The Bodger and pulled A.L.F.I.E Lever 'WHITE MAN'S GRAVE.'

The atmosphere grew close and humid. The Bodger felt sweat forming under his shirt. The air was filled with the bedlam cacophony of a tropical rain forest at dusk. Baboons howled in the distance. Night birds cackled and hooted. Somewhere, a leopard coughed. George de Beetle's ears tingled to the shrilling of a million nocturnal insects as he forced his malaria-racked fingers to write the last message of the doomed expedition on a grimy piece of cartridge paper; the feeble light of a candle illuminated the yellow Mepacrin-tinged features, the six weeks' growth of beard and the ragged khaki shirt of the last survivor while he recorded the discovery for which six men had died; the message would be put in a bottle and floated down the Amazon so that the world might one day know the true fate of Colonel George de Beetle and his gallant companions.

'. . . Hypodermic syringes, Admiralty pattern number 421, are now obsolete and should be returned to base depots. B.R. 1334(47) will be amended in due course . . .'

The Bodger stood and watched like a child at a fairground while George de Beetle worked through his morning's programme composing, among many other items, a massive column of Nietzsche rhetoric for the Director of Gunnery Division, a wittily-turned barb worthy of Wilde himself for the Hydrographer of the Navy and a morceau for the Head

78

of Fleet Work Study which might have been a fragment from a poem written by a world-weary mandarin and floated downstream upon a lotus blossom. When The Bodger left George de Beetle's office he felt humbled, as though he had been privileged for a short time to watch the processes of genius at work. He now saw George de Beetle, not as a tiny grey man, faceless, a typical civil servant, but as probably the most prodigious literary giant the world had ever seen and his office, not as a miserable hutch in which one of the anonymous thousands earned his yearly salary, but as a literary Valhalla to which pilgrimages would no doubt be made after George de Beetle's death.

* * *

It was nearly five o'clock before George Dewberry came in with the evening papers.

'This is the four o'clock edition, sir. It's not mentioned in the earlier ones.'

The Bodger ripped a newspaper from George Dewberry's hands and ran his eyes hungrily over the front page. '*Where is it?*' he hissed.

'It's on the back page, sir. Small paragraph at the bottom.'

The Bodger read the whole paragraph almost at one glance. It was, nearly verbatim, the noncommittal statement The Bodger himself had written. There were no headlines, no innuendoes and no embellishments. A small fire had broken out in HMS *Octopus*. That was all. A peace which passes all understanding descended upon The Bodger. Just as he was putting the paper down, he noticed the Stop Press.

'PONTEFRACT! Saints in torment, I forgot all about me Little Black Bikini!'

There it was, before his eyes. 'Pontefract. 3.30. Little

Black Bikini (8–1) 1; Octane (5–4 fav.) 2; Chivalry (100–9) 3. ½l. 2l. 8 ran.'

'Eight to one,' breathed The Bodger. '*Forty quid!*' The heady bouquet of a successful *coup*, that pungent perfume for which a gambler will sell all he owns, rose to The Bodger's nostrils. He read the result over and over again, whispering the words. 'First, Little Black Bikini, eight to one, second Octane, five to four favourite, third Chivalry a hundred to nine, half a length, two lengths, eight ran.' The Bodger repeated the stanzas as though declaiming an heroic poem.

George Dewberry, a veteran backer of horses, recognised the danger signals. Unless he was very much mistaken, his superior officer was showing every symptom of a bout of gambling fever and as this was probably the first time he had contracted the disease, the attack was likely to be a severe one.

'Congratulations, sir,' George Dewberry said, cautiously. He remembered reading somewhere that he ought to reassure the patient in a loud, cheerful voice. 'I expect you'll ...'

'... Two lengths, eight ran,' murmured The Bodger. He shook himself and George Dewberry was relieved to see The Bodger looking at him with sane, normal eyes again.

'That's a good win to open your account with, sir.'

'Isn't it?' said The Bodger gleefully.

'Let's hope the next win is on Battlewagon.'

'My God yes,' said The Bodger. 'I'm looking forward to that trial!'

6

The Bodger and Julia picked up George Dewberry outside his digs in the Cromwell Road at eight o'clock on Sunday morning. George Dewberry was looking dishevelled and liverish.

'Hop in, George,' said The Bodger. 'God, you look like the dog's dinner.'

'I went to the "Denmark" last night, sir, and I fell among friends. We finished up drinking Cointreau and soda at four o'clock this morning.'

'Cointreau and soda.' The Bodger grimaced. 'It makes me feel old just to think about it. Julia darling, this is George Dewberry, one of the poor unfortunates I once trained when he was a cadet.'

'How do you do, George,' said Julia. 'There's some coffee in a flask, if you'd like some.'

'Thank you, I'd love some,' George Dewberry said gratefully. He tried hard not to goggle at Julia. Even at this hour of the morning, Julia was worth looking at. Her black hair was caught in a white Alice band, her eyes were wide and hazel-coloured, and her complexion was as smooth and creamy as a magnolia blossom. George Dewberry knew very little about English women, having had only a few desultory girl-friends, but he recognised a perfect specimen when he saw one. Julia was wearing a light grey tweed costume of which George could only see the cape coat but she looked altogether the kind of woman George would not have minded marrying himself.

'Now I shall have to step on it,' said The Bodger, 'or Poggles will be champing at the bit, like one of his horses.'

Poggles was waiting by the gallops, surrounded by what appeared to be half the population of Newbury. It seemed that the whole stable, from the head lad down to the youngest stable lad and all their relations, had turned out to watch Battlewagon's trial.

'Julia, you're looking as glamorous as ever,' Poggles said.

'You're looking very fit yourself, Peter.'

'Ah, it's all this fresh air and freedom from worry, I don't think. But you haven't met my wife Melanie. Darling, I'd like you to meet Julia Badger and her wicked husband. You can call him Bodger.'

Melanie was a very healthy-looking girl with a fresh complexion and rosy cheeks; compared with Julia she was the primrose to the orchid. She was evidently used to conditions underfoot on the gallops. She was wearing a stout pair of wellington boots, a tweed skirt and a sheepskin-lined leather jacket.

'It's very good of you to slog all the way out here to see this horse, Melanie,' The Bodger said.

'My goodness,' said Melanie, 'I wasn't going to miss this! It's not every day we get a Derby runner in action.'

'He's not a Derby runner, yet,' Poggles said, sourly.

'Don't be such an old sourpuss, darling. Of *course* he's a Derby runner!'

'By the way, Poggles,' The Bodger remembered something he had meant to say. 'Very many thanks for the tip about Little Black Bikini.'

'You had something on her?' Poggles beamed. 'I thought she had a chance but of course you can never be sure.'

'I won forty quid on that nag.'

Poggles blinked. 'Blimey, you *have* been bitten by the bug!'

'Robert, you didn't tell me about this,' said Julia accusingly.

'Very wise too,' said Poggles. 'What the ear don't hear the heart don't worry about.'

'But supposing it lost!'

'Julia my dear, racehorses *never* lose,' Poggles said firmly. 'They only fade away.'

'Ready now, Guv'nor,' called the head lad.

'Thank you, Josh.' Poggles turned to The Bodger. 'We've done our best by your wonder-horse. I've put three other very good horses, August Hill, Glissade and Nimonic, in with him. August Hill is a four-year-old and he's about the best handicapper we've got in the stable. He's earned his money every year he's been in training and he's a thoroughly good, genuine, down-to-earth runner. Glissade is actually a Classic filly. She was sixth in the Oaks this year, in fact at one stage we thought she was going to win. She won at Newmarket early this season and she won again over a mile at Ascot. She's going to stud at the end of the year. Nimonic is one of our most promising two-year-olds. I wish to God *he* was entered for the Derby instead of Battlewagon. He won at Chester and he was only beaten a neck by Slavonic Dancer at Goodwood and he's our main hope for the Timeform Gold Cup next month, though I don't expect he'll make much impression on La Petite if she runs.'

An air of expectation had settled on the spectators. Every head was turned towards the start of the gallop, just out of sight over the hill.

'The trial will be over seven furlongs and I've told them to come along at a good pace until they reach me and then quicken for the last furlong. Three of the local jockeys have come in to ride August Hill, Glissade and Nimonic and I've got Tommy Sparling, who's actually our first stable jockey, to come down from Newmarket to ride Battlewagon. I've told Tommy to bring Battlewagon along with the others but if he gets tired to let him drop back. I don't want him to blow up. If we knock hell out of him today he might never show any interest in racing again. They're carrying weight for age, which means that Nimonic and the wonder-horse are at level weights, Glissade is giving them about a stone and a half, and August Hill is giving them about two stone. They should be jumping off any minute now.'

The Bodger looked down the gallop. There was a hint of mist in the distance but the hazy blue sky promised a perfect autumn day. The air was clean but had a bite in it as a reminder of winter. The Bodger took a deep breath and decided that there were few other things he would prefer to be doing than standing where he was, waiting for racehorses to gallop by. He was about to make some comment to this effect when a glance at Poggles' tense face quelled him. With sudden insight The Bodger guessed that this was no ordinary trial for Poggles. Poggles had been very near the truth when he had accused The Bodger of treating horse-racing as a new and fascinating pastime. It might be a pastime for The Bodger but for Poggles and his stable it was deadly serious. The chance of having a Derby winner in the stable, no matter how remote that chance might be, was a matter of terrible gravity. That was why Poggles had arranged this trial, disregarding the fact that it was Sunday and he and his stable had already worked a full week; that was why the three local jockeys had given up Sunday morning with their families and Tommy Sparling had travelled all the way from Newmarket to ride the horses; and that was why the whole stable staff were here now watching in a taut silence. Where the Derby was concerned, all other considerations were dismissed; it was such a race that no trainer, owner, or jockey would hesitate to snatch at the least shred of a chance of winning it. The Bodger mentally saluted such dedication and kept a respectful silence.

'Here they come.'

The horses had appeared over the brow of the hill. They had split into two pairs. Battlewagon was in the leading pair, moving easily and giving every sign that he was enjoying the morning's proceedings.

'Who's that with him?'

'Glissade.'

As the horses galloped nearer it became clear to all that the jockeys on August Hill and Nimonic were already hard at work to bring their horses along at the pace set by Glissade and Battlewagon.

'At least he's keeping up with them,' said The Bodger.

'He's doing more than that, *damn you*,' muttered Poggles with unusual ferocity. 'Keep quiet, Bodger.'

Fifty yards from where Poggles was standing, the jockey on Glissade took out his whip and sent her ahead whereupon Battlewagon reached out strongly and in a few strides was level with her again. As they passed the trainer August Hill, Nimonic and Glissade were all under pressure, indeed were being hard ridden, while Tommy Sparling on Battlewagon was still sitting as imperturbably as a Buddhist effigy, having not moved a muscle; even The Bodger could see that the grey's relentless stride was galloping the others into the ground. The horses passed on with a ragged beat of hooves towards the end of the gallop, leaving The Bodger a vivid impression, like a clear-cut cameo, of the horses' billowing white breath, the crouched figures and rhythmic whip movements of the jockeys, and the set face and motionless body of Tommy Sparling on Battlewagon.

Long after the buzzing of conversation and the exclamations

of '*Did* you *see* that grey!' had begun all around him, Poggles still stared up the gallop where the jockeys had dismounted and the stable lads were walking the horses round.

'That's odd,' he whispered. 'That's *very* odd. That's *extraordinary! Why* hasn't he done that before?'

'I said there was something there, Guv,' said the head lad. 'He was playin' with that filly. She's not in his class.'

Poggles did not answer but set off at a rapid walk towards the horses. Holding on to their hats, The Bodger and George Dewberry followed.

By the time The Bodger had caught him up, Poggles was already busy in conversation with Tommy Sparling. Listening to them, The Bodger once more felt chastened. He had just seen a thrilling gallop by four racehorses. Poggles and Tommy Sparling had seen much more; they had seen a complex exercise, a demonstration of a dozen points of stride, balance, temperament, stamina and handling which had to be examined and assessed. Each point had to be weighed and its significance estimated. For the first time since he had burst into the world of racing The Bodger had an inkling of the true extent of his ignorance.

Tommy Sparling touched his cap with his whip. He was a tiny bowed man with a face having the same colour and knobby contours as a walnut. 'Not a bad horse you've got there, sir,' he said to George Dewberry. 'Dunno about the *Derby*, but he should win a couple of races for you.'

'I hope so,' George Dewberry said. 'Though we've got our eye on the Derby.'

'Let's go home and have a drink,' said Poggles. 'Before we start getting ambitious. One trial doesn't make a Derby winner.'

'That shook you, didn't it, Pete?' said Melanie, when they reached the house.

'It did. He's never done anything like that before. He must have known you were watching, Bodger. What are you going to have?'

'Seeing as how what a great day it's been, I think a large glass of whisky will be the answer, Poggles. There's only one thing worrying me now.'

'What's that?'

'I don't think you're going to have room for Battlewagon's picture on your wall!'

'Don't you worry, Bodger. We'll make room if we have to.'

Among the photographs and paintings of racehorses, hunters and ponies which seemed to cover every inch of the living-room walls, The Bodger noticed a water-colour of a chestnut colt. The painting was amateurish but the artist had succeeded in capturing some quality in the horse which attracted The Bodger's attention; it was the quality which in a full-grown stallion a racing man would have called 'presence'.

'Who's this, Poggles?'

'Maximist. By Donatello out of Anathema, by Nearco. Melanie did that picture of him. You remember him, George, your aunt was very fond of him.'

'I remember him very well.'

'We called him Maxie,' said Melanie. 'I think he was the horse I liked more than any other.'

Poggles gave The Bodger his glass of whisky. 'He was going to win the Derby for George's aunt. The best colt we ever had here. He was going to be the champion to end all champions. But he broke a leg on the gallops one morning. It happened right in front of me. That leg broke with a crack I'll hear to my dying day. The leg was just dangling loosely.'

'Oh how terrible,' said Julia sympathetically.

87

'The worst part was that he still had his head up and his ears pricked. He could see the other horses carrying on and he was itching to go with them. But of course he never did that, ever again . . .'

'The children were watching,' Melanie broke in, 'and Peter wanted them to go home so they wouldn't see what was going to happen but I said no, it was good for them to see it. Teach them that it wasn't all patting and sugar lumps. I wish I hadn't. They've never forgotten it.'

'. . . We still get drama and tears from Alice, our youngest daughter, whenever anyone mentions Maxie. I dashed home and got the gun and he *knew*, you know. That horse knew what I was going to do. The look he gave me. I put my jacket over his head and shot him.'

'Oh how *terrible* for you,' said Julia, the tears springing into her eyes.

'Never mind.' Poggles bit his lip. 'Cheers, Bodger. I suppose after what happened this morning, nothing will dissuade you and George from becoming racehorse owners?'

'I'm still willing,' The Bodger said. 'How about you, George?'

'*I'm* still game,' said George Dewberry stoutly.

'Let me first give you a few facts and figures. This is something I say to all new owners I've had here. Not that it's ever prevented them rushing upon their fate! What I'm trying to say is this – in any given season there are between four and five thousand racehorses in training for the flat. Let's say for the sake of argument there are four thousand five hundred. I can tell you that of those horses only two out of five will win any sort of race at all during the season, and only one in ten will win enough in stake money to pay for its keep. I know you read in the newspapers how such and such a horse has won thirty or forty thousand pounds in the season but take my word for it you can count those horses virtually on the fingers of one hand. You can safely say that during the average season one horse in a hundred will win more than five thousand pounds and only one horse in ten will even pay for the food it eats! You can look it up, if you don't believe me. It's all in *Ruff's*.'

'I believe you,' said The Bodger devoutly. 'How much does it cost to keep a racehorse then?'

'The cost of keeping one horse in training for one year in a stable like mine,' Poggles said deliberately, giving each word emphasis, 'is approximately one thousand pounds.'

'A thousand a year!' shouted The Bodger. 'Hellzapoppin man, what d'you feed 'em on, five pound notes or something!'

'Just about,' said Poggles, grinning. 'Actually we feed 'em on oats, bran and hay mostly. Your horse likes the odd bottle of milk stout occasionally.'

'Does he?' The more The Bodger heard about him, the more Battlewagon was beginning to appear a horse after The Bodger's own heart.

'That thousand a year doesn't only cover food. That takes in my fees, the vet's fees, jockeys' fees, the blacksmith, transport, a reasonable amount of forfeit money, insurance and tips to the stable lads. And of course it presupposes that the horse is not going to win a race.'

'Which you think very probable in this case?'

'I didn't say that, Bodger.'

'Your face said it for you!'

'Well, you never know, there are over two thousand races in the Calendar. We ought to be able to find *one* he can win.'

'There's only one race I'm interested in.'

Poggles groaned and looked despairingly up at the ceiling.

'The main thing is, sir,' said George Dewberry, who had

finished his glass of whisky and was hoping for another. 'Are we going to go on with this?'

'Well,' The Bodger said, 'this puts a different complexion on matters. That's five hundred a year each. People live on that. Can't we have lots of people sharing the expenses?'

'Only four,' said Poggles. 'You can't have more than four in a partnership in a horse.'

'Why not?'

'Because the Jockey Club say not.'

'*I'd* like to join in,' Julia said, suddenly. 'I've got some money of my own and you've obviously set your heart on this, Robert darling. I'll take one share.'

'That's splendid Julia, thank you,' said The Bodger, much moved. 'That still leaves one share . . .'

There was a moment's silence. They all looked at Poggles, who ran his fingers frantically through his hair. 'All *right*. Since *nothing* I've said seems to have had the slightest effect... If you can't beat 'em, join 'em. I must remember to make an appointment with my psychiatrist because I certainly do need my head examined . . . I'll take the other share.'

'Bravo darling!' Melanie clapped her hands. 'If you hadn't said that *I* was going to.'

'Then we *all* need our heads examined,' complained Poggles. 'Have another drink, George.'

'Why, thank you. That went down without touching the sides. I'm beginning to feel better every minute. I must be careful not to over-correct, though. Now that we've settled that, hadn't we better choose some racing colours?'

'Let's have something *really* exotic!' said The Bodger. 'How about fuchsia with green spots, silver sleeves and a Cameron tartan cap?'

'. . . With a beer tankard rampant back and front,' suggested George Dewberry.

'All right then, let's have straw whisky, pink champagne sleeves and a rich ruby red port cap . . .'

'Just one word,' Poggles put in warningly. 'Remember you're dealing with the Jockey Club here. They're every bit as stuffy an organisation as the Admiralty. The Stewards of the Jockey Club and Their Lordships have a great deal in common. When either of them makes a decision it all happens rather like the mating of elephants: everything goes on at a very high level, there's a lot of smoke and dust, and nothing happens for several years. I think Julia ought to choose the colours. What d'you think, Julia?'

'I'd like something very simple,' said Julia. 'And I think red, white and blue is a good combination. How about Navy blue, white sleeves and a red cap?'

'Just the job!' said Poggles. 'I'll put them up to Weatherby's and if they approve we'll have them registered. Leave all the paperwork to me. We're all agreed then? All four of us are equal partners in this horse and he'll run under the colours of Mrs R. B. Badger which *are* – Navy blue, white sleeves and a red cap.'

'Right,' said The Bodger.

'Right,' said George Dewberry.

'Right,' said Julia.

'We shall now drink to Battlewagon and the Derby!'

They all raised their glasses.

'We seem to have organised this like a military operation,' Melanie said.

'Operation Blue Riband,' Julia said, on an impulse.

'To Operation Blue Riband!'

'. . . And I need my poor head looked at,' added Poggles.

7

The Bodger was never able to discover where or how the news of Operation Blue Riband leaked into the Ministry of Political Warfare. The Bodger's intention had been to release the story of Battlewagon to the press when the time was ripe, probably a few weeks before the Derby. But this modest aim was speedily made obsolete. The first intimation The Bodger had that Operation Blue Riband had already swelled beyond its original frame-work came, inevitably, from The Tatler and Bystander who passed The Bodger in the corridor, paused long enough to whisper 'Heard the buzz, Bodger? Operation Blue Riband!' and hurried on.

While The Bodger was still pondering the implications of The Tatler and Bystander's remark, Jim Sewter of the Amalgamated Press Bureau rang up.

'What can you tell me about Operation Blue Riband, Bodger?'

Knowing that a little information went a long way with someone of Jim Sewter's calibre, The Bodger metaphorically kicked for touch. 'I can't tell you much about it at this stage, Jim. It's still very much at the planning stage.'

'It's a new scheme, isn't it?'

'I suppose you could call it that.'

'A New Deal, in fact?'

'Oh, I wouldn't go as far as *that!*'

'Come on Bodger, don't be so cagey. We give the Navy good space as well as bad, you know. Particularly if we get some co-operation.'

The Bodger could not help himself responding to the blackmail. 'I suppose you could just stretch a point and call it a New Deal.'

'Thanks very much, Bodger.'

The Bodger hoped that he had succeeded in leaving Operation Blue Riband so vaguely defined that even Jim Sewter would be unable to use it. The next morning's papers showed that he had been too optimistic. Two papers carried front-page pieces on Operation Blue Riband, one in the form of a swingeing attack on the Army and the other a virulent assault on the RAF. The Bodger read them with a mixture of alarm and glee.

The first piece was short but explosive. 'Wake Up, You Brasshats! Just when recruiting figures are sinking to their lowest ebb since the war, the Navy today announce a comprehensive scheme of pay, family welfare and benefits for the ordinary matelot designed to put the sailor on equal footing with a civilian. It's a New Deal for the Navy and its code name is "Blue Riband." Well done, the Senior Service! In the meantime, what are the Sam-Browned denizens of the Rip van Winkle War Office doing for the ordinary tommy? Nothing! We say – find the guilty men! Publish their names! Sack them! Sack them!'

The Bodger smothered an involuntary giggle. 'Cor blimey,' he said to himself, 'that'll put the cat among the pigeons and no mistake!' He turned to the second item, which was directed at the RAF. It began: 'Navy First – The Rest Nowhere! A brilliant breakthrough in electronics technology has just been completed by Admiralty scientists. The new process, known as New Deal, involves a complete reshuffle of thought in electronics. Technical experts estimate that the new operation, code-named Blue Riband, has put the Navy ten years ahead of its rival services in the field of guided weapons. When asked about Operation Blue Riband, an official Air Ministry spokesman said: 'Never heard of it.' The RAF is our most costly armed service. We say to them – "Gentlemen, you *should* have heard of it!" We say – Get out of your air force blue ivory tower and see what the Navy are doing! We say to the RAF – "You've been left at the post again!"''

The Bodger's heart went out to the unknown 'official Air Ministry spokesman.' 'Probably some poor bastard like me,' he thought sympathetically.

If The Bodger had needed any further proof that Operation Blue Riband had burst its bonds and was now running free, Geoff Pinner provided it in The Vaults at lunch time.

'Cap'n! Let me buy you a drink!'

'If you insist. I'll have a large whisky.'

'Coming up! You know matie, you're a cunning one.'

'What do you mean by that?'

'I *said* you were in the wrong trade. You coming here and asking *me* for advice and all the time you were cooking up "Operation Blue Riband"!'

'You think it's good?'

'*Good!* Cap'n, it's the best stunt since Barnum and Bailey! It's a rave! It's a sure sell-out! When I think of you standing here at this bar and saying you didn't know anything about advertising! I can take a joke and this time the joke's on me! Let's get to business.'

'Business!'

'*Yes.* When Solly read the papers this morning . . .'

'Who's Solly?'

'The boss. When he read the papers this morning and I said I knew you, he said two words. He only said two words. Know what they were?'

'No?'

'Get him. Get him, he said. How soon can you get out of the Navy, Cap'n?'

'Hold on a minute now! I'm not leaving the Navy just yet!'

'Two thousand a year . . .'

'No.'

'*Three* thousand a year!'

'No.'

'Expenses . . .'

'No.'

'Car . . .'

'No.'

'*Two* cars!'

'Not for half a dozen cars.'

'I can't shake you?'

'No.'

'I won't say you're wrong, Cap'n. If you carry on this way you'll be able to go to Solly and name your own price.'

'I haven't any intention of going to Solly.'

'You know where to come when you leave the Navy!'

'I'll bear it in mind.'

The Bodger returned to his office quite buoyed up both by Geoff Pinner's whisky and by his enthusiasm. George Dewberry was waiting for him.

'The Admiral wants to see you, sir.'

The Bodger's smile faded. 'What's he want?'

'I don't know, sir. I imagine it's about Operation Blue Riband.'

'I imagine so, too. Stay here will you, George? I want to see you when I come back. *If* I come back.'

'Best of luck, sir.'

Admiral Gilpin was still in the position where The Bodger

95

had last seen him, crouched cross-legged on top of his desk, contemplating his gothic horror-fiction state board.

'That you, Badger?'

'Yes, sir.'

'Operation Blue Riband.'

'Yes, sir?'

'How's it going?'

'Very well sir, in the circumstances.'

'I don't know what you mean by that, Badger, and I'm not going to enquire. You know my own views about publicity for the Royal Navy, Badger. I won't repeat them. But I happen to have just had lunch with the Sixth Sea Lord, Admiral Sir Seamus Dogpit, and I'm asked to inform you that the Admiral is very impressed by the progress you've made with Operation Blue Riband. I may say, between ourselves, that the Sixth Sea Lord has not had such a good opportunity of wiping the eyes of the Army and the RAF since he took up the appointment. I myself am not in favour but I thought you had a right to know that the Admiral is very pleased.'

'Thank you, sir.'

'What fuel are they using?'

'What fuel, sir? Oh, carbohydrates, sir. The normal organic substances.' The Bodger remembered the odd bottle of milk stout. 'Plus alcohol, of course, sir.'

'When will they be ready?'

'We hope to be ready for full power next June, sir.'

'Not till then?'

The Bodger decided to abandon the last vestiges of caution and let Operation Blue Riband rip. 'We shall be having partial repair and calibration runs before then, sir.'

'Good. Keep me informed, Badger.'

'Aye aye, sir.'

The Bodger made his way unsteadily back to his office, constantly feeling the walls to counteract the eerie sensation of unreality which was attacking him like the onset of vertigo. George Dewberry was still waiting anxiously.

'How did it go, sir?'

'He told me that he and the Sixth Sea Lord are very bucked about Operation Blue Riband.' The Bodger looked appealingly at George Dewberry. 'George, what are we going to do about this?'

'I don't know, sir.'

'We just can't tell everybody the truth now. The whole thing's gone too far. I don't think they'd *believe* me, in any case, even if I did tell them. Everybody seems to be convinced that Operation Blue Riband is the biggest thing to hit the Navy since they took up steam.'

'We'll just have to do a Brer Rabbit, sir. Lie low and say nuffin until it all blows over. These crazes don't normally last very long.'

But George Dewberry had badly underestimated Operation Blue Riband's staying powers. The word spread like a brush fire. Minute sheets by the thousand were circulated. The effects of Operation Blue Riband were felt in the farthest limits of the Navy. Stores officers sitting at peace in their chairs in Singapore were catapulted to their feet by urgent demands marked 'Operation Blue Riband.' Ships off the coast of South America received dynamic signals diverting them to take part in Operation Blue Riband. Excited wireless operators in the remotest parts of the globe listened in to an evergrowing volume of traffic relating to Operation Blue Riband. At home, the Army and the RAF were driven to defend themselves against attacks of increasing viciousness. Norman Beetleford began to work overtime.

Norman Beetleford's official title was 'General Public

Liaison Officer to the Ministry of Political Warfare.' His office performed the functions of an Admiralty Complaints Department. When a lady wrote to the Admiralty complaining that her stockings had been ruined during Navy Days, the letter was passed to Norman Beetleford. When a Gloucestershire angler threatened to sue the Admiralty because the nuclear submarine which had been seen to leap the weir had ruined all the fishing, it was Norman Beetleford who smoothed the incident over. The General Public Liaison Office was a convenient dumping-ground for all inconvenient correspondence and the letters received there were a useful gauge of the climate of public opinion on the Navy. Norman Beetleford normally presided over his department with unruffled tranquillity; his answering letters were models of suave good manners and unshakeable courtesy. But when The Bodger called on him, three days after the news of Operation Blue Riband broke, Norman Beetleford was looking like a fugitive from a chain gang and was actually in the act of taking two aspirins in a tooth-glass of water.

'Has everyone gone mad, Bodger?' he said. 'My mail normally runs to half a bag a day. In the last two days it's gone up to six bags twice a day!'

'You mean Operation Blue Riband?' The Bodger said guiltily.

'Of course I mean bloody Blue Riband! Everybody's got it on the brain! I've just been answering a letter from a man who claims that he's in hospital because he fell down an open man-hole while reading about Operation Blue Riband in his newspaper, and what are the Admiralty going to do about it? And here's a letter from an old lady in Bettws-y-Coed who tells me she's just seen an advertisement for Blue Riband bird seed and is it any good? Bird seed, I ask you!'

Everyone in the Department was fully occupied on Operation Blue Riband. Frank Bethell, the editor of *What?*, was lying full length on his office floor, firing .22 bullets from a range of ten feet at test panes of armoured glass. 'It's for Operation Blue Riband,' he explained to The Bodger.

Admiralty Archie was in a flux of activity. 'He's working on something for Operation Blue Riband,' Bert Beattle told The Bodger.

When The Bodger noticed that he had not seen Pat FitzBeetle for a couple of days, he was told that Pat Fitz-Beetle, Ted Beetlebotham and Danny Beetelsen were on location in the Bahamas shooting material for a feature on Operation Blue Riband.

'They're shouting for an AFO on Operation Blue Riband, Bodger,' George de Beetle said. 'What d'you want me to say about it?'

'Go easy on it, George,' The Bodger said. 'It's still pretty hush-hush, you know. Can you make it vague?'

'I can make it anyway you like.'

'Make it look as if you're saying a lot without actually saying anything. Can you do that?'

'Of course.'

George de Beetle placed a top hat on his head, took a battered red dispatch case from a drawer, and rang a small division bell vigorously. The authoritative chimes of Big Ben rang through the office as George de Beetle pressed A.L.F.I.E Button 'GOVERNMENT WHITE PAPER' and began work.

Ten days after Battlewagon's trial, Operation Blue Riband was self-supporting and self-generating. It would keep all parties happy for another six months without any further prompting from The Bodger. It seemed that quite by accident The Bodger had created the touchstone which had eluded Jimmy Forster-Jones and all his predecessors. Operation Blue Riband had the magical properties historically associated with the Genie of the Lamp. It took whatever shape a man desired of it. Like the Derby itself, it was a chimera, a product of wishful thinking; as The Bodger had claimed for the Navy in his ill-fated poster, it was all things to all men. To the Tatler and Bystander it had been a fresh piece of gossip, to Jim Sewter the chance of a scoop, and to Geoff Pinner it was the perfect publicity stunt. George de Beetle, that neutral man, had treated Operation Blue Riband as just another brief, but Bert Beattle had looked upon it as something intriguing for Admiralty Archie to think about. Pat FitzBeetle had seized on it as a golden chance to take a holiday in the West Indies, while Admiral Dogpit had welcomed it as a unique opportunity of scoring off the Army and the RAF.

The only people who were not happy about Operation Blue Riband were The Bodger and Norman Beetleford. Norman Beetleford solved his immediate problem by succumbing to a nervous breakdown and being admitted to a sanatorium but The Bodger was left, with George Dewberry, to carry the burden of an uneasy conspirator. They lived from day to day expecting the façade of Operation Blue Riband to be penetrated and the whole structure of it to vanish as quickly as it had risen.

Their narrowest escape was the surprise visit paid by Sir James Beetleburgh, the Permanent Secretary. The Bodger was given no time to warn his Department and George Dewberry was still operating the teleprinter when The Bodger ushered Sir James into his office. George Dewberry stopped the machine as Sir James peered down at the tape.

'Lucky Alphonse II? What's that mean?'

'Lucky Alphonse II is the name of a big fleet exercise next

spring, Sir James,' The Bodger explained. 'This is a machine for composing code-names. You see, Sir James, we can't make them up ourselves or we'd give ourselves away. Our selections would begin to show a pattern after a time. One man would tend to choose the names of flowers, another man would tend to choose the names of towns. It's the same with numbers and letters for cryptographic purposes, Sir James. If one person continues to choose them, no matter how random he tries to be he'll show up a personal pattern after a period of time. If you let him go on long enough eventually he'll compromise the system.'

'Is that so?' said Sir James Beetleburgh, with interest. 'Did this machine think of Blue Riband?'

'Oh yes, Sir James.'

Sir James Beetleburgh passed onwards, an expression of bewilderment on his face. George Dewberry restarted the teleprinter which resumed its clattering message.

'. . . Lucky Alphonse II beat Poor Yorick (gave 8lb) by 2 lengths at Nottingham (7f.) August 2nd. Golden Bowler was out of first 6 to September Song (rec. 3lb) at Newmarket (6f.) July . . .'

8

The unaccustomed sensation of being an accredited race-horse owner (Poggles had telephoned that the new partner-ship and Julia's racing colours had appeared in the *Racing Calendar*) caused The Bodger, for the first time in his life, to study the racing press. The racing page, with the details of the runners and riders at the meetings of the day, had hitherto been a section of his morning paper which The Bodger had always skipped over, along with the woman's page and the situations vacant, but now that he had come to look at the subject more closely The Bodger realised that he had been depriving himself of a great deal of entertaining reading. In almost every daily and Sunday newspaper and in several weekly magazines there were columns of well-informed comment and opinions on racing which, in The Bodger's opinion, were of a higher standard of writing than that covering any other sport except, perhaps, cricket.

The Bodger was charmed by the pseudonyms chosen by the fraternity of racing correspondents. A dull minority referred to themselves as Course Correspondents but the majority had aliases of a rare and exciting originality. The Bodger made the acquaintance of such bizarre characters as Master Herbert, Hotspur, Gimcrack and Kettledrum. Then there was the military brigade – Captain Heath, Captain Keen and Winco; the nobility, represented by The Marquis, The Duke, Marlborough, and Sir Harry; the omnipresent Man On The Spot; the omniscient Newsboy; the many-eyed Argus; the lynx-eyed Scout; the doughty Audax; the mischievous Robin Goodfellow; and the cunning Bird-catcher. All, day by day, provided The Bodger with a never-failing source of entertainment.

Before The Bodger could get the maximum benefit from the racing press he had first to learn racing argot, that *lingua franca* with which the racing correspondent titillated as well as instructed his readers. For example, a horse was never described merely as being urged to run faster – it improved, it was sent ahead, reminded, shaken up, given the office, asked the question, or set alight. Similarly, no horse ever did anything so pedestrian as win a race – it scored, it obliged, it landed the odds, justified confidence, opened its trainer's account, delighted its connections, proved itself to be a gentleman, or was the medium of a successful gamble.

Diverting though the racing fraternity were on the subject of winning horses, they reserved their most inspired flights of language for horses which lost. After studying several hundred reports in detail, The Bodger came to the conclusion that no horse in the history of racing had ever *lost* a race. Any animal which failed to pass the winning post in front of the others in the same race had sweated away its chance in the paddock, lost its chance at the gate, was not too generous, proved too much for the lad to handle, had swallowed its tongue, found the trip too short/too long, did not have a clear run, could not act on the firm/soft going, or became unbalanced at a critical stage. However (The Bodger was invariably consoled) the horse had not been disgraced by the showing, would be all the better for the outing, and should be watched next time out.

'George, why didn't someone tell me about these splendid fellows before? There's a laugh a line here.'

'They vary a lot, sir. Some of them write very well but give very bad horses. The best ones keep up an average of somewhere between one and two winners out of every three nap selections. That would be all right, provided you knew which one out of the three it was going to be, but some of them have very long losing runs. Like jockeys.'

'Aren't there systems for backing winners, George?' said The Bodger. 'I once served with a Captain who was a racing fiend. He was always covering the chart table with his selections. He used to calculate the state of the moon, and the first letter of the horse's name, and add in the date and so on.'

'There are systems, sir,' said George Dewberry disparagingly. 'Hundreds of 'em. Bert Beattle once got Admiralty Archie to work some of them out. Archie thought deeply about it and came to the conclusion that if you follow any system correctly, back every horse the system indicates, and refrain from any horse the system doesn't indicate, if you follow it exactly and conscientiously, sooner or later you'll lose all your money.'

'How disappointing. But to get back to this tipping business. I can understand these newspaper chappies. It must be quite a strain to pick a horse for every race, every day, but it's part of the newspaper's service, like the book reviews, or the film critic, or the motoring bloke. What I *cannot* understand are these professional tipsters. If their information is so good why don't they just slip quietly away, *back* the horse, and retire for life?'

'Ah, there you've asked the question you must never ask, sir. I don't know what the solution is. There seem to be plenty of them so there must be some money in it. It may be they rely on a stream of fresh clients all the time. I don't know.'

'Talking of tipping, George, what have you got for today?'

'I don't fancy anything for today, sir. But the Middle Park Stakes *tomorrow* . . .'

'You needn't tell me what to back tomorrow! There's a very good horse running. What's it called, now?'

'Battlewagon, sir?'

'That's it!'

'Have you ever been to Newmarket, sir?'

'Never in me life,' said The Bodger. 'What's the course like?'

'In a way there's no such thing as *the* Newmarket course, as such. They've got dozens of courses. They've got about twenty they never even use nowadays, from the Beacon course which is about four miles, down to the Exeter course which is about six furlongs. Even now, they've got the Rowley Mile, which is part of Across the Flat, the Cesarewitch Course which joins on the end of the Rowley Mile at an angle, the July Course, which starts on the Cesarewitch Course and goes off at another angle. And now they've got the Sefton Course which goes round in circles between the two. Then there are all sorts of permutations and combinations of the courses, the Dewhurst Stakes Course, the Rous Course, the Bunbury Mile, the Chesterfield Course, and the Suffolk Stakes Course. I often wonder how the jockeys work out which is which. It's rather a pity you're starting off there, sir.'

'Why is that?'

'It's really a connoisseur's course. You can't see much of the racing until they're inside the last two furlongs. Everybody there is always an expert. You find that everyone round you has always backed the winner and you haven't. And there's always a bitter wind blowing straight from

Siberia into your teeth. It may be a splendid test of a racehorse but I'm afraid it's not my idea of my favourite course by a long way.'

*   *   *

Newmarket was much as George Dewberry had described it to The Bodger. A wind from the steppes of Russia was blowing across the Heath and the swept contours of the land and the enduring shapes of the trees on the racecourse road suggested that the same wind had been blowing for centuries. It was a raw October afternoon and The Bodger felt sorry for the jockeys in their thin silks as the winners of the first two races were enthusiastically roared home by a crowd which consisted of one-third Army officers in plain clothes, one-third grey-faced men in raincoats and cloth caps, and one-third comfortable, homely middle-aged women whom The Bodger supposed were on a Women's Institute outing.

The Bodger, self-conscious about the owner's badge in his lapel, Julia, self-assured in a new hat, and George Dewberry, self-confident with a good half-bottle of whisky safely under his belt and a full flask in his overcoat pocket, joined Poggles as he was saddling Battlewagon for the Middle Park Stakes. Poggles was wearing a tan-coloured short raincoat and the well-kneaded brown trilby of a veteran race-goer. Battlewagon looked a picture. Even The Bodger's inexpert eye could see that the horse was ready to run for its life.

'How is he, Poggles?'

'He's eaten up and he's raring to go. But of course he always is. I've never met a horse look more as though he enjoyed race meetings.'

'Is that a good sign?'

106

'All depends. It isn't if it means he enjoys watching the other horses race, and that's all he's done up to now.'

'Do you think he stands a chance, Peter?' Julia asked.

Poggles shrugged. 'On *paper* he's got a very good chance, Julia. If he runs like he did the other day, he should go close. He beat Nimonic by two lengths which is about equivalent to six pounds and Nimonic took Slavonic Dancer to a neck at Goodwood. On that form Battlewagon is about four or five pounds better than Slavonic Dancer who looks as though he's going to start favourite today. What beats me though is that somebody was watching that trial the other day. Somebody always is, no matter how hard you try to keep it secret, and we didn't try very hard. Somebody must have seen him and yet the ring will take any money you like to offer at fifty to one. Obviously the ring are not impressed. Look at that board over there.'

There was an indicator board standing by the tote building nearest to the paddock; on it columns showed the amount of money being laid on the horses on the tote, represented by approximately equivalent odds on the book. Two columns on numbers five and seven, either side of Battle-wagon, showed towering totals while above Battlewagon's number, six, the column had barely lifted itself off the base line. The Bodger looked at his race card; numbers five and seven were Slavonic Dancer and a horse called Chemotaxis.

'It's just the same round the back,' said Poggles.

The Bodger nodded. He remembered passing the main indicator board behind the stands where the numbers of units betted on Slavonic Dancer and Chemotaxis had been flicking up faster than the eye could read them. Battle-wagon's total had remained static for minutes at a time, giving only the occasional desultory movement denoting the investment of some optimistic speculator who either through natural perversity or hereditary masochism persisted in backing hopeless outsiders.

Poggles felt round Battlewagon's saddle one ultimate time, ran his fingers down inside the girths, slapped the horse on the shoulder and nodded to the stable lad.

'Take him away, Jimmy. Keep walking all the time. Don't stop for a moment. I don't want him to get the idea this is his annual outing to see his cousins!'

'I don't know about you, Poggles,' said The Bodger, 'but I'm going to have something on our horse. It may be bad but it's not all that bad.'

The Bodger side-stepped through the throng of rain-coated men who were hovering round the bookmakers' steps, waiting to rush forward and overwhelm the book-makers with bets just before the off.

'Five bob each way, Battlewagon.'

The bookie, a lean cadaverous man with a look of permanently-soured disillusionment, took in The Bodger and his owner's badge.

'Don't take dollars,' he said disdainfully.

'All right, make it a pound . . . No, make it a fiver each way!' By God, thought The Bodger, I'll take that look off his face.

'Two hundred and fifty pounds to five, sixty-two and a half to five a place,' the bookmaker said to his clerk, as though imparting good news. He whipped a ticket off the pack, gave it to The Bodger, and accepted The Bodger's money. The wraith of a smile passed across his granite face.

'I'll just put that here,' he said, tucking The Bodger's money in a waistcoat pocket. 'Come in useful against me old age.'

'Don't you worry, I'll be back,' The Bodger promised.

'I'll be waiting,' said the bookmaker.

When The Bodger returned the horses were all in the parade ring and the owners and trainers were standing in groups keeping their faces impassive against the concentrated stares of the crowd round the rails, as though one careless grin or confident gesture at this point could bring the price of a horse plummeting downwards.

'Look,' said Julia, 'there's another grey, just like Battle-wagon.'

'Abernotherone,' said Poggles. 'By Abernant, out of Closing Time. Horrible pun, but it's not a bad horse.'

The Bodger was less interested in the horses than in their owners. 'You know,' he said, 'there must be a special milliner somewhere who makes hats for women racehorse owners. Probably some blacksmith in Newmarket here who turns them up on his anvil.'

'Thank you, darling,' said Julia sweetly.

Poggles plunged in where St Michael himself might have been excused some hesitation. 'You don't count, Julia,' he said. 'I see what you mean, Bodger.'

The Bodger and Poggles gazed, with respect, at Chemo-taxis's owner, who was a small fat woman, with a figure like a man's thumb. Her face was invisible underneath a chinese coolie-type hat (three foot in diameter) which was secured by a pin the size of a skean dhu. The wind was catching her hat and tilting her body so that she progressed everywhere in a sideways manner, looking like a mushroom in a high wind.

'That's Madeleine Brotherhood,' Poggles said. 'Her brother Sir Leonard owns La Petite.'

Chemotaxis's trainer was dressed in sombre black. He was a gloomy-looking man with pouchy, grey cheeks which were engraved with lines of care; he looked like an archbishop gnawed by a secret worm. Twice he stopped his horse, felt its off foreleg, and then looked up at the sky, as though imploring Allah to be merciful.

'Don't be fooled by that,' said Poggles. 'That horse is as fit as a flea.'

The next group included the owner and trainer of a wiry chestnut called Brash. The owner was a willowy woman wearing a grey mink coat which fell in the shape of a pyramid from her shoulders. Her hat was a breath-taking pylon of purple straw topped by an artificial rose. The Bodger estimated that the height of the artificial rose, from masthead to ground, was a shade over eight feet.

The trainer was a chunky man with a weathered, brick-red complexion. His suit was a baggy pepper-and-salt tweed but he had a beautiful red carnation in his buttonhole. His brown trilby looked as though at some time in the past he had tried unsuccessfully to cultivate penicillin upon it. From time to time, for no visible or audible reason, he tossed his head back and guffawed defiantly at the clouds, daring Jehovah to do his worst.

The jockeys came out in single file to join their owners and trainers. Tommy Sparling's nutty face wore a confident grin as he approached. It was the first time that Julia's colours had been worn in anger on a racecourse and The Bodger thought them uncommonly smart.

'Now,' said George Dewberry. 'Now I'll know something I've always wanted to know. *What* do they say to the jockey when they're out in the middle here. I've always suspected that they were telling him the joke for the day.'

'. . . You know the horse better than I do Tommy,' Poggles was saying. 'Make your best way home. If you can. He's a genuine stayer but his idea of staying means staying at the back. You may have to shake him up early.'

The signal was given to mount. Poggles gave Tommy

Sparling his leg up. Tommy settled himself in the saddle, held the reins and whip together. 'See you over there, sir,' he said to The Bodger, inclining his head towards the winner's enclosure.

'He means the car park,' Poggles said acidly.

Chemotaxis's jockey's instructions were evidently more comprehensive than Tommy Sparling's. Madeleine Brotherhood and the archepiscopal trainer were both talking at once. The jockey, an apprentice, a fresh-faced, pink-cheeked lad who looked about fourteen years old, was glancing from one face to the other like a tennis umpire and was nodding and smiling politely.

'I doubt if he's paying all that much attention,' said Poggles. 'He's a bright lad, that apprentice. He's going to go places. I'll lay you a pound to a penny he's got his own ideas of how he's going to ride. Let's go up to the stand.'

Tommy Sparling brought Battlewagon at a swinging clip past the stands on his way down to the start. Tommy Sparling held him on a short rein but Battlewagon was stepping out nicely. The Bodger's heart swelled with pride and affection.

'He looks good, doesn't he?' he said.

'It's not going down that counts,' said Poggles cynically. 'It's coming back.'

'Who's that jockey going down now, with his arse sticking out?'

Poggles looked furtively over his shoulder. 'Bodger,' he said uneasily, 'do try and moderate your voice to a dull roar. That's the champion jockey.'

'I think my nerves call for a quick medicinal slug,' said George Dewberry, getting his flask out of his pocket.

'For Christ sake, George, not here!' said Poggles. 'You'll have the Stewards chucking you out and I'll never live it down.'

'I'm sorry,' mumbled George, 'I'm used to being in Tatts.'

'They're under starter's orders,' said the loudspeaker.

Looking through his binoculars (borrowed from the hall porter) The Bodger could see that the starter was having difficulty in lining up his field.

'There's one horse giving trouble,' he said. 'Why don't they say who it is?'

'They're not allowed to.'

'Why ever not?'

'Because the Jockey Club say not. I can tell you who it is anyway. It's Brazzaville.'

'*They're off!*'

Battlewagon jumped off smartly with the rest. He had been drawn in the middle of the course and when the field split into two, attached himself to the group racing on the stands side which was led as far as the Bushes by Magistrate and Sepulchre. On the far side, Brash led from Slavonic Dancer and Chemotaxis. Three furlongs from home, the running on the stands side was taken up by Brazzaville, with Battlewagon still in the rear of the group but galloping as though he intended to show them all a thing or two. Brash still led on the far side but Poggles, watching through glasses, fancied that his jockey was already beginning to look anxious. In spite of that, Brash had opened up a lead of two lengths two furlongs out and led from Chemotaxis and Abernotherone. Going into the Dip, the apprentice on Chemotaxis took out his whip and the horse moved smoothly up to Brash's quarters. A hundred yards from the line the race was between Chemotaxis and Brash, with Abernotherone improving rapidly. In the last few yards Chemotaxis sprinted away from the field and won by a length and a half, leaving a tired Brash to beat Abernotherone, finishing like an express train, for second place. Slavonic Dancer was fourth, another half a length away. Battlewagon, still running as though the afternoon's racing had been devised for his benefit, made no show in spite of Tommy Sparling's best efforts, and finished equal last, next to a friendly bay colt called Lapsus Linguae.

Poggles let his binoculars drop to the extent of their cord. 'Ah well, I suppose I didn't really expect anything else,' he said, in a voice which betrayed that he was bitterly wounded and disappointed.

Poggles was curious to see how The Bodger and Julia would react to Battlewagon's debacle. Poggles could remember past races when owners who were paying a thousand a year, or a sizeable fraction of it, had been rewarded by the spectacle of their horses running nearer last than first and Poggles had been the recipient of some hard, harsh words. George Dewberry, Poggles could see, was in a state of whisky-induced euphoria where he would not have been perturbed to see his horse bucking up the course backwards waving his tail in the air but (though it was true that one at least of Poggles' owners was just as objectionable when winning as when losing) Poggles well knew that a moment like this was the acid test of the average owner. Poggles turned to The Bodger and Julia and was taken aback to see them both grinning at him.

'Cheer up, Peter,' said Julia. 'There's always another race another day.'

'Wipe that smile off your face, Poggles,' said The Bodger. 'Anyone would think you expected that horse to win.'

Poggles puffed out his cheeks. 'I'm glad you're taking it that way,' he said. 'I admit that I expected him to do better than that, whatever I may have said about him.'

'Here is the result of the last race,' said the loudspeaker. 'First, number seven, Chemotaxis. Second, number seventeen, Brash. Third ...' the voice faltered. 'Number six, Battlewagon?'

Poggles started. 'The judge has made a mistake! Hold on a minute!'

Poggles dashed away. There followed a confused period when neither The Bodger nor Julia could fathom what was happening, which culminated in the words 'Weighed in' over the loudspeaker. Poggles dashed back.

'I've never known that happen before! The judge thought the grey was Battlewagon! The colours are fairly similar. I've *never* known that happen before!'

'Can't he change it?' said Julia.

'Not as far as the betting is concerned. Not now the numbers are up in the frame and the blue flag's been hoisted. Cor, what a turn-up for the book!'

'Does that mean we can collect some money?' said The Bodger.

'Of course! How much did you have on?'

'A fiver each way.'

'Cor stone me, you *have* got the bug, haven't you, Bodger? Let's see, at fifty to one, quarter the odds a place, minus your stake, you've won fifty seven pounds ten!'

'I'm looking forward to collecting it, too,' said The Bodger.

'Bodger, you were obviously born dead lucky. And there's obviously something funny peculiar about that horse of ours.'

9

'Dead lucky yesterday, sir,' the hall porter said to The Bodger in the morning.

'It was, rather.'

'That horse don't seem much good, sir, does it?'

'He'll be all the better for the outing,' said The Bodger. 'He'll be worth watching next time out.'

'I may watch him sir, but I won't back him.'

The news that there had been a setback to Operation Blue Riband infiltrated the whole Ministry and was reflected in The Bodger's own department. Frank Bethell had increased the calibre of his bullets to .303. 'I've struck a snag,' he told The Bodger.

Bert Beattle restarted Admiralty Archie on the abandoned refitting and maintenance programme. 'There's a hitch on the Blue Riband stuff, so I'm told,' he said, 'so I've gone back to the refitting cycle project until they get it sorted out. That was a good idea of yours, Bodger, and I've taken it a stage further. I find I get much better results if I cut the theoretical number of ships and days at sea to a quarter. It looks very promising.'

A sun-tanned Pat FitzBeetle reappeared in the office. 'We were recalled,' he explained to The Bodger. 'We got back last night. It seems there's a hold-up on the Blue Riband material so we had to come back to consolidate. It's a shame, just when Danny and I were getting the hang of the limbo dance.'

Admiral Gilpin sent for The Bodger.

'What's happened to Blue Riband? The Sixth Sea Lord tells me you've had a set-back.'

'It's true the first full power trial didn't go quite as well as we'd hoped, sir,' said The Bodger.

'I'm not interested in failures, Badger. The Army are getting cocky again.'

'I'm sorry, sir.'

'I expect more effort, Badger.'

'Aye aye sir.'

Strangely, the danger which The Bodger had feared most did not materialise. When Jim Sewter next telephoned, to confirm the story that Indian hemp was being grown on a commercial scale on a naval air station in Suffolk, he showed no interest in Operation Blue Riband. The Bodger himself had to raise the subject.

'Aren't you interested in Blue Riband any more, Jim?' he asked.

'No. As far as we're concerned that story's dead. Unless you can produce some scandal on it?'

'No, I can't do that,' said The Bodger hastily. 'But I just wondered if you wanted a progress report.'

'We're not interested in things progressing. We cover beginnings and endings, the more dramatic the better. Thanks for the gen on the reefers, Badger. See you.'

It was significant that The Bodger had anticipated the marijuana story and had already prepared the facts in a suitable statement for the press. It was a sign that The Bodger was beginning to learn his job, that he was growing more confident every day in his dealings with the press. He had lost the defensive tone in his voice when speaking to reporters and had even managed to throw off his suspicion that they were all against him. He had discovered that there had been much truth in George Dewberry's words to him on his first day at the office. The press, The Bodger discovered, lived from hour to hour. They were too impatient to concern themselves with sensibilities; they had to have news, they had to have it fast and they had to have it right. Once The Bodger had accustomed himself to providing the facts, providing them fast and providing them right, he found his relations with the press improving remarkably. After a few weeks, The Bodger even felt confident enough to telephone Jim Scwter himself.

'Jim, you know that story you called me about this morning?'

'The divorce case, you mean?'

'Yes. I wonder if you could let it down lightly . . .'

'Now, Bodger . . .'

'Jim, that man joined the Navy with me . . .'

'Bodger, *nobody* wants their names in the papers. *Everybody's* got friends who'll read all about it. They should have thought of that before they did it . . .'

'I know, I know, I quite see that, Jim, but I don't think the news value of this story is big enough to justify the harm it will do . . .'

'With all due respect Bodger, you're not the man to judge that. The more harm done, the bigger the story, surely.'

'Yes,' said The Bodger despondently, 'I suppose so.'

'It's not up to me anyway, it's up to the editors. But I'll see what I can do. O.K.?'

The Bodger was relieved and gratified to see that only one paper mentioned the case, in a tiny paragraph, though he was not naïve enough to suppose that his conversation with Jim Sewter had been wholly or even partly responsible for the story's exclusion; The Bodger was often surprised by the apparent haphazardness with which the press selected their stories. Many stories over which The Bodger had pondered for a long time, carefully weighing what he should say and what he should omit, and which he had finally released with misgivings, had never appeared in the newspapers at all. Other stories which The Bodger had thought hardly worth a telephone call had sometimes made the front page. Jim Sewter had an explanation for the phenomenon.

'All news is news, Bodger,' he said. 'But some news is more news than other news. Get it?'

As The Bodger warmed to his job, his difficulties with the press diminished, but his difficulties with serving officers remained constant. The attitude of serving officers towards the press swung violently between two opposite poles and The Bodger could never make up his mind which of them made his job the harder. There were officers, normally young, keen, and firm believers in the value of a good press, who embarrassed The Bodger by giving unauthorised and free-for-all press interviews at which everything was on the record; and there were older, staider officers, brought up in the tradition that the only good naval officer was a silent one, on whom the mere mention of the word 'Press' reacted like a bee-sting and whom The Bodger had the greatest difficulty in convincing that, however bad a story might appear at first-hand, it would appear immeasurably worse if reported from a distance. Between these two extremes lay a vast population of officers who, when approached about providing press facilities, said they were prepared to deal with it but hoped it would never happen, like a mutiny. All officers, however, joined in pouring invective upon The Bodger's head.

'Why are you asking all these questions?' complained the captain of a frigate which had narrowly missed the Royal Yacht in thick fog. 'I thought you were supposed to be on our side.'

'I *am* on your side, dear boy,' The Bodger said, patiently. 'But I've got to tell the press *something*. I'm trying to make the best of what happened and if I don't *know* what happened, how can I make the best of it?'

'All right,' said the frigate captain, grudgingly. 'What happened was this. *He* was going *far* too fast . . .'

Not all The Bodger's problems were naval ones.

'Bodger *dulling*,' breathed the Fashion Editor of *Woman and Garden*, 'we're doing a feature on the new sailor necks and could we bring the gels down to one of your divine ships, dulling, and have some sweet sailors draped over the guns . . .'

'Hold it hold it, Cynthia! Do I take it you want to bring some models down to one of our ships, is that it?'

'Dulling Bodger, you're so quick!'

'I'm afraid I can't arrange that sort of thing from here, Cynthia.'

'Oh Bodger,' The Bodger could almost hear Cynthia pouting, 'I thought you could arrange anything . . .'

'Most things, Cynthia, but not this. What I *could* do is give you the names of a couple of ships in Portsmouth and you could write to their captains . . .'

'*Portsmouth!* Dulling, that would be like going *abroad!*'

'Can't help it, Cynthia. There's no ship coming to London till next year. How would a submarine suit you?'

'A submarine! Dulling, how dangerous! The gels would be terrified!'

'That's up to them, but if you like I can give you several submarines. You can mention my name and say I said they were to give you *every* facility.'

'Dulling, what ever can you mean?'

It seemed that anyone and everyone who wanted information on the Navy was directed to The Bodger's telephone.

During an average working day The Bodger answered calls from scoutmasters, the Royal Institute for the Blind, solicitors, schools' careers masters, editors of technical magazines, the BBC, philatelists, the British Medical Association, film producers, the Foreign Office and the Soldiers, Sailors and Airmen's Families' Association. The Bodger battled gamely with these callers for some time before he became aware that he had in his own department one of the world's foremost authorities on all matters connected with ships, the sea, and the Navy.

Jake van der Beetle was the Curator of the Naval Historical and Maritime Museum. He was also a Fellow of the Royal Society, the Royal Geographical Society and the Royal Historical Society. He was a regular contributor to several learned journals of restricted circulation as well as such publications as *The Connoisseur*, *The New Scientist*, *History*, and *Popular Boating*. He was frequently away from his office, travelling to New London, Stockholm and Melbourne to lecture on ship-building methods of antiquity, the influence of the Phoenicians on Mediterranean colonisation, or the use of monitors during the American Civil War. He was a quiet, donnish man who wore a white goatee beard and, when he was in his office, a yellow linen coat. Whenever The Bodger called on him he was invariably studying some object on behalf of a correspondent, perhaps a shapeless piece of salt-stained wood to determine whether it could once have been part of a Roman galley, or a glass eye to decide whether it could have been that worn by the Bosun of the *Formidable* during the Battle of the Saints Passage.

'At least it's not supposed to be Nelson's eye,' he said to The Bodger, taking his watchmaker's glass out of his own eye. 'That makes a change. People seem to have a fixation about Nelson. About seventy-five per cent of the work I do is connected with him. Here's the latest.'

Jake handed The Bodger a limp hank of coarse brown hair.

'What's that?'

'That is reputedly a lock of Nelson's hair. The man who sent it to me has a theory that Nelson was not killed at Trafalgar at all but was cold-bloodedly murdered by Hardy, who poisoned him with arsenic. He asks me to decide how old Nelson was when the hair was taken from his head and to test it for arsenic.'

'And is there arsenic in it?'

'Oh yes. A good deal of it.'

'You're not trying to tell me Nelson *was* murdered by arsenical poisoning?' cried The Bodger, already wondering how he could keep J. Sewter off the story.

'Not necessarily,' said Jake, cautiously. 'This happens to be horse hair.'

'Thank God for that!'

Much impressed by Jake van der Beetle's knowledge and erudition, The Bodger was walking back to his office when he passed a narrow, dim corridor he had never noticed before. The Bodger stopped. At the end of the corridor was a small, green door. Feeling that he was about to cross the threshold of the normal world into Alice's Wonderland, The Bodger knocked.

The sensation that he had trespassed from the paths trodden by human beings and wandered into a fantastic existence of nursery rhyme and fable was heightened when The Bodger straightened up after stepping through the door and found himself in what appeared to be a fabulous menagerie. To his right were the shadowy figures of a griffin, a wyvern and a phoenix in earnest conversation. To his left a unicorn, a mermaid and a sphinx regarded The Bodger with an unvarying, inimical stare. A light glowed above an easel at the far end of the room, illuminating a man in a green smock and gleaming on rows of medallions round the walls. The Bodger recognised the dragon of China, the lion of Ethiopia, the chrysanthemum of Japan and the elephant of Siam; there were the star of David, the sun of Apollo, Cancer and Capricorn, a formation of silver martlets, a blue field studded with golden fleur de lys, the white rose of York, a pelican with its pierced breast, and ranks of heraldic and national emblems. The Bodger was in the presence of someone of whom he had heard but never met, Mr Desmond Esmond Drumbeetle, OBE, Master of Naval Heraldry, sometimes known irreverently in the Department as Beetle King of Arms.

Beetle King of Arms was a man of imposing presence. He had the polished manner of a diplomat and the haughty, swarthy face and cruel stare of a Spanish conquistador; he might have been Foreign Secretary to Francisco Pizarro.

'How good of you to call, Badger,' he said.

'I'm sorry I haven't been before,' said The Bodger. 'Can I look?'

Beetle King of Arms swept The Bodger towards the easel with a courteous gesture of his long, elegant hand. The Bodger walked round the easel and then stopped, as though a pike had been thrust through his heart.

The picture was not finished, several parts were still sketched in pencil, but there was enough complete for The Bodger to see on the easel an extraordinary likeness of Battlewagon.

'It's a symbol for Operation Blue Riband.'

'What made you choose that?' The Bodger asked, in a choked voice.

'A racehorse? It had to be a racehorse. With a name like Blue Riband, it's obvious, isn't it?'

'But why a grey?'

'More presence. More feeling. A grey is so much more dramatic than a chestnut or a bay. It had to be a grey. He'll have a jockey when he's finished.'

'What colours?'

'One must be patriotic. I thought red, white and blue would be suitable. Rather trite but, as I say, patriotic.'

Looking at Beetle King of Arms' Blue Riband motif, The Bodger knew without any doubt that if that picture of a grey racehorse once escaped from the room, his secret would be out. The coincidence would be too great.

'You did know that Operation Blue Riband had met with a serious delay, didn't you?'

'No, I didn't. Has it?'

'Yes. A great pity. The whole thing's been shelved temporarily, I'm afraid.'

'Does that mean I've got to go back to designing ships' crests?' Beetle King of Arms spoke as though ships' crests were his equivalent of the salt-mines.

The Bodger shook his head. 'It looks like it, I'm sorry to say. I should put that under wraps for the time being. I'll let you know when Blue Riband is on the way again.'

'Oh dear.'

The disappointment in Beetle King of Arms' voice wrung The Bodger's heart strings. However, he hardened his heart.

'Doesn't this sort of thing have to go through lots of committees before it's decided?'

Quite unwittingly, The Bodger had touched Beetle King of Arms' guilty conscience.

'They do. But you know, I just thought I'd have a go at it . . .'

'I should keep it quiet, if I were you,' said The Bodger sternly, realising his advantage. 'I'll let you know how things turn out.'

'Thank you,' said Beetle King of Arms, gratefully. He hung a cloth over the picture of the racehorse. When The Bodger left him, he had picked up a small wooden hippopotamus and was gazing at it mournfully.

The Bodger hurried back to his office, blessing the chance that had made him stop at the little green door. Beetle King of Arms' inspired reasoning had been too close to home for The Bodger's peace of mind. It occurred to The Bodger that he might inquire after the progress of the real Operation Blue Riband.

'Morning, Poggles, how's the wonder horse?'

'Still wondering,' said Poggles. 'When I last saw him he was just staring vacantly at the bulkhead of his box.'

'Poggles, there was something I wanted to ask you. I know so bloody little about horses and stables and all that. I wondered if I could come down to your place and do a short acquaint course.'

'You want to come down and look round the stables?'

'Yes, if that's all right.'

'Of course. Come whenever you like.'

'Don't you start at some God-awful hour in the morning?'

'There's no need for you to be there then, Bodger. Get here about eleven in the morning. The second lot should be pulling out about then.'

'Right. And Poggles . . .'

'Yes?'

'I'd like to do some riding, if I could. After all, if I'm going to be a racehorse owner I might as well know something about it.'

'Cor chase the crows round the 'ouses, this *is* a changed

Bodger! Who was it who told me many years ago that he only knew two things about a horse, and one of them was rather coarse?'

'That's just it, Poggles! That's what I want to change.'

'All right. On your own head be it,' said Poggles, prophetically.

10

'Are you going to ride dressed like that, Bodger?' asked Poggles, looking doubtfully at The Bodger's dark grey business suit and bowler hat.

'Of course. Why, should I have brought me cycle clips or something?'

'If I were you I'd change. I've got an old pair of trousers and a sweater in the office. I should wear those.'

'If you insist, Poggles.'

When The Bodger emerged from the office, wearing a pair of brown corduroy trousers and a dark wine-coloured sweater, he said: 'If you don't mind, I'll keep my bowler on, just in case of accidents.'

'Very wise,' said Poggles. 'I've had Elsie saddled up for you, Bodger. She's nice and quiet and she'll give you a pleasant ride.'

Elsie was an eleven-year-old brown mare with a white blaze and one white forefoot. She was used as a stable hack and was occasionally hunted by Melanie. She was a polite and placid animal and, having first put her ears forward and inspected The Bodger, she seemed reconciled to his company for the day.

Jimmy Bones, who was Battlewagon's stable lad, stood waiting to give The Bodger a leg up. The other stable lads gathered round, nudging each other and speaking out of the sides of their mouths.

'When you get up, take a look forrard and if you can see two ears you know you're on the right way round, Bodger,' Poggles said, helpfully.

'Yok, yok, yok,' said the stable lads appreciatively.

The Bodger looked at Elsie's back. Now that he was so close, the saddle did seem to be a remarkable distance from the deck.

'Grab the saddle, put your left leg in Jimmy's hand and push downwards.'

It was much easier than The Bodger had expected. In no time he found himself riding high in the saddle, his feet in the stirrups and the reins in his hands. Elsie stood submissively still, her eyes widening a little at the unusual distribution of The Bodger's weight on her back.

'Now, sit properly in the saddle. Get a good grip of the reins. Make sure your feet are comfortable in the stirrups.'

Josh, Poggles' head lad, had already sized up The Bodger's physique and stepped forward to adjust the stirrup leathers.

'How do I start her up?' said The Bodger.

'When you want to go ahead just kick gently. Pull the starboard rein when you want to go to starboard and the port rein when you want to go to port. Not too hard, she's got a good mouth. When you want to stop, pull both.'

'How do I go astern?'

'Don't worry about going astern. Just concentrate on going ahead. Ready?'

'Yes,' said The Bodger.

Poggles and Josh mounted expertly. 'Right,' said Poggles. 'Let go forrard.'

'Let go aft,' said The Bodger.

'Slow ahead together,' said Poggles.

The Bodger kicked experimentally and to his delight Elsie, rightly construing the convulsive movement of The Bodger's foot as a wish to go on, walked forward. Poggles and Josh followed. The small cavalcade, led by The Bodger, began to move out of the yard.

The stable lads, who had been watching The Bodger's equestrianism with the closest interest, waited until The Bodger and Elsie were just passing them and then began to click their teeth and utter guttural noises.

The sounds seemed to disturb Elsie. She laid her ears back, kicked out one rear leg in irritation, and slewed sideways. The Bodger attempted vainly to correct this unexpected over-steer.

'Cut that out!' roared Poggles.

'Get back to it!' bellowed Josh.

The stable lads scattered. Elsie quietened. The Bodger recovered his composure.

'I'm sorry about that, Bodger,' said Poggles. 'They're always a bit cheeky with newcomers. There's Melanie.'

Melanie was watching from the house. She opened the living-room window and called to The Bodger. 'Look after my mare, won't you, Bodger?'

'It's the other way round, Melanie! She'll have to look after me!'

The Bodger thought riding a very sociable means of progression. Elsie knew the lane up to the gallops blind-folded and The Bodger could safely trust her to find her way, leaving him free for conversation. The motion was soothing, the view of the countryside was unexpected, and the feeling of superiority caused by being on horseback instead of on foot was very comforting. The Bodger approved of riding.

'Have you ever ridden before, Bodger?' Poggles asked.

'I used to ride a pony when I was about ten years old. I even used to go hunting on it. If you can call it hunting. I used to get to the meet all right and touch me cap to the Master as they do in all the best hunts. But then someone would give a great yell or blow a trumpet or something and they'd all dash off and vanish! How do I look now?'

'Ace,' said Poggles, with conviction. 'I dig that crazy bowler.'

'What's the programme today, Poggles?'

'I thought we'd go up to the gallops first and watch the second lot working and then come back here and I'll show you round the stables. What did you want to see particularly?'

'Everything.'

'Crikey, that's a tall order. I'll show you what I can but there's not a lot going on now. This is the tag end of the season. There's only the Cambridgeshire tomorrow and the Manchester November Handicap next month left of the big races. That's the lot till next March. We shall have a few hurdlers but that's all. We've got August Hill in the Manchester one.'

'Has he got a chance?'

'Quite good.'

'Perhaps he'll make up for Nimonic the other day.'

Poggles gestured carelessly. 'I wasn't very disappointed about that. Nimonic's a good horse on a racecourse, mind you, but he's no match for La Petite. Our only hope was that she might have an off-day.'

'That must be quite a filly.'

'She's a bloody racing machine,' said Poggles.

'What's she done this season?'

'She's been well raced. She's had six races and won 'em all, by shorter odds and longer distances each time. First time on a racecourse she won the Fitzwilliam Stakes at Newmarket. She started at twenty to one and won by a neck. Then she went to Chester and won the Lily Agnes Stakes, starting at five to one and winning by half a length. From there she went to Ascot and won the Queen Mary Stakes. She started at nine to two and won by two clear lengths. By this time people were really beginning to sit up and take notice and when she went to Goodwood for the Molecomb Stakes she was a hot favourite. I think she started at even money but anyway she doddled it. By the time the Cheveley Park Stakes came round it was a job to find a bookie to lay her. They asked for a hundred to thirty and she beat the rest of the field out of sight. That brings us up to date to the Timeform Gold Cup and our own hopeful Nimonic. She's won over thirty-five thousand quid as a two-year-old and that's a record by a long way. They could retire her to stud now and make a packet out of her but Sir Leonard's got his eye on the Classics. I'm told he's even thinking in terms of the Derby. It's difficult to believe she's related to Battlewagon, isn't it?'

'Is he having another race this season?'

'No, I'm putting him by for the winter. Unless you feel you want more for your money?'

'Good heavens, no. You're the expert.'

Poggles smiled grimly. 'You've no idea how refreshing it is to hear you say that. I've got some owners who want their horses to run even though I tell them it will ruin the animal for life. I'm getting cold. Let's trot a bit.'

'How do I do that?'

'Oh, just jog up and down in time to the music.'

Elsie was only too ready to trot. She started forward at the first touch of The Bodger's heels and soon The Bodger was jogging up and down, more or less in rhythm, behind Poggles.

'I'm not sure this isn't the time of year I like best of all,' said Poggles, when they paused at the top of the gallop.

'Even better than the spring?'

'I think so. It all looks so incredibly clean now.'

Most of the trees beside the gallop had lost their leaves

and the countryside had taken on its winter shape. The day
was clear and The Bodger could distinguish the fine filigree
of the branches in the trees at the bottom of the gallop and
the individual furrows in the field beyond more than a mile
away. The Bodger felt the cold on his hands and the warmth
of the mare through his thighs and smelt the odour of saddle
leather and an elusive autumnal scent compounded of wood-
smoke, dried leaves and hoar frost on the grass. He looked
down the broad vista of the gallop and felt an urge to whip
Elsie up and gallop until they were both exhausted.

'Fine life you lead, Poggles,' he said wistfully.

'All right if you're a fresh air fiend.'

Poggles took up his position halfway down the gallop and
soon the horses came in sight, cantering in single file.

'Not going so fast today?' said The Bodger.

'They're only cantering. All these horses are in full
training. You don't want to gallop them just for the sake
of it. Everybody seems to think racehorses go flat out everywhere. That's quite wrong. Some horses need a lot of work,
a good gallop twice or three times a week. Others are quite
all right with cantering. It varies a lot. Once you've got a
horse's windpipe clear and he's put on lots of muscle you
may find he only needs to gallop when he's on the racecourse.

'The secret is to keep them so they *want* their food and
want to race. Otherwise you might find you've left all your
best races behind on the gallops at home.'

The horses swung by, one by one. The stable lads, conscious that the Guv'nor's eye was upon them, were all riding
correctly, with their knees and elbows in and their backs
straight. The Bodger was surprised at their motley dress.
For some reason he had expected the stable lads to be
dressed uniformly but they were wearing corduroys, blue
jeans, stained grey flannels, sweaters, ragged sports coats,

and windcheaters. Poggles recited the horses' names as they went past, occasionally bellowing at them when the lads showed signs of bunching together.

'. . . King of Winter . . . Windrush . . . Your friend Little Black Bikini, Bodger . . . August Hill . . . Asmodeus . . . Counter Pixy . . . Keep spaced out there, blast you!'

'I don't know how you tell the difference between them, Poggles, honestly. I mean I can tell the difference between a bay and a chestnut, just about, but not between two chestnuts. Not at this distance.'

'Believe me, Bodger, if your bread and butter depended on noticing the least little thing wrong with them, you'd know the difference between them.'

When the last horse had cantered through, The Bodger said: 'Can I have a go at galloping?'

'Not on a racehorse you can't.'

'No, I mean on Elsie.'

'I don't see why not. Go down to the end of the gallop, and when I drop my hand, jump off and come as fast as you can past us. We'll see how you get on. Don't worry about Elsie, she won't let you go too fast.'

The Bodger trotted down the gallop, turned round and faced Poggles. Elsie stood restlessly, shifting her weight from one side to the other. This was something unusual. Plainly she had been asked to look after a madman for the day. She had no idea what he wanted of her but it was obviously something new and Elsie welcomed it. Anything was better than just standing about.

Poggles' hand dropped. The Bodger shook the reins, kicked, and was away. Once Elsie understood what was required of her, she responded enthusiastically. The Bodger felt the mare gather her strength and accelerate underneath him. Soon The Bodger was hanging on without knowing how, his body jolted by the pounding, his eyes streaming tears, his mouth shouting wordless cries of encouragement and his whole being rejoicing in a spasm of reckless joy and release.

The intoxication of the gallop rose to The Bodger's head. He went too far. Just beyond Poggles a line of hurdles began. The Bodger steered Elsie towards the first of them.

By now convinced that she was in charge of a lunatic but being an experienced hunter and a confident jumper, Elsie headed for the hurdle, paused, expecting the signal kicks to begin her jump, received no sign, collected herself and leaped the hurdle like a stag.

The Bodger's share of the partnership was less successful. Totally ignorant of the magnitude and relative directions of the forces involved when a horse jumped an obstacle and quite unprepared for the tremendous piston-like drive of Elsie's hindlegs, The Bodger lost reins, stirrups and seat and was boosted into short-lived orbit.

The Bodger rose into the air still in a sitting position, as though ejected from a pilot's seat, and landed on his hands and knees. His bowler fell off his head and rolled on the ground. When Poggles and Josh reached him, The Bodger was still crouched on his hands and knees, apparently reading the maker's label inside his bowler hat.

'You all right, Bodger?'

The Bodger lifted his head. 'By God,' he said sincerely, 'that was marvellous!'

'The first thing to do now is climb right back on again.'

'I'll do just that. Come here, gel.'

Elsie had been quietly cropping grass a few yards away but came up willingly. As The Bodger struggled up on to her back, she bared her teeth and snorted.

'You know what she's saying?' said Poggles. 'She's saying

"They say you can't come without the 'orse but brother you can't come without the rider either!" Never mind Bodger, nobody can call himself a horseman till he's fallen off many times!'

When they reached the yard again, The Bodger said: 'What happens to Elsie now?'

'One of the lads will do her. Wipe her down and brush her.'

'Hadn't I better do it? After all, I rode her.'

'Why, yes,' said Poggles, a tiny flicker of respect coming into his eyes, 'if you want to.'

Josh showed The Bodger how to remove the saddle and bridle and tie up the horse. Meanwhile, the word had spread round the stables.

'Ey,' said the stable lads, one to the other, 'that —— owner is goin' to —— do —— Elsie!'

A crowd gathered round Elsie's box. The Bodger pushed up his sleeves and took a piece of soft sacking from Josh.

'Where do I start?'

'Anywhere,' said Poggles. 'As the actress said to the bishop.'

The stable lads threw back their heads and laughed like demons.

The Bodger considered the question and then laid a tentative hand against Elsie's side. Elsie started at the unfamiliar touch and gave vent to a shrill affronted whinny. The Bodger withdrew his hand quickly. The stable lads stamped their feet and howled.

'Keep at it, Bodger,' said Poggles encouragingly. 'She's only saying "Go on, I like it!"'

'Is she? I thought she was saying "If you touch me there again, I'll scream!"'

The stable lads howled again. This was better than the television.

Gaining confidence, The Bodger began to scrub Elsie with the wadding. Poggles gave advice from time to time. 'Work away from the head ... Now the feet ... Don't forget her ears ... Stand close when you do underneath her so she can't wallop you ... Careful ...'

After the wadding came the body brush and the curry comb. The body brush was an ordinary-looking brush like a floor brush but the curry comb was a peculiar oblong piece of metal studded with spikes.

'Like a fakir's ashtray,' said The Bodger.

Josh showed The Bodger how to use the body brush and how to clean it every so often by rubbing it across the curry comb. The Bodger had not been working with the body brush for long before he took off his sweater and rolled up his shirt sleeves. Doing a horse was warmer work than it looked.

'Knockers,' cried the stable lads, knowingly, 'knockers.'

'What's that mean?' asked The Bodger.

'It means you go to the door of the box and knock your curry comb on the deck. If you've been doing it properly you should get a small amount of dust from it.'

The Bodger knocked out his curry comb and was gratified by a puff of grey dust.

'You'll make a stable lad yet, sir,' Josh grunted.

When it was all over and The Bodger had rolled down his sleeves and put his sweater on again, Poggles said: 'I'm rather glad you did that, Bodger. It's good for morale.'

'I enjoyed it.'

'Let's go and have a drink.'

'How I need one,' said The Bodger fervently.

'How did you get on Bodger?' asked Melanie, after waiting tactfully while The Bodger put down his first pint of beer without pausing for breath.

'By golly, that was good,' said The Bodger, wiping his mouth. 'How did I get on? I fell off.'

'Oh dear.'

'It wasn't Elsie's fault. It was mine.'

'He put Elsie at that bottom line of hurdles,' said Poggles.

'But they're four feet high!'

'Is that all?' said The Bodger. 'It felt as though I'd been shot about twenty feet into the air.'

'It always feels like that,' said Poggles. 'I doubt if you were more than six feet off the ground at any time.'

'Did you hurt yourself?' Melanie asked anxiously.

'No fear,' said The Bodger.

Poggles chuckled. 'He landed like an Olympic pole-vaulter, darling. I've never seen anything like it. Josh said "Give him to me for six months and he'll make a rider." That's a compliment, Bodger. Old Josh has got a pretty poor opinion of owners in general.'

'That *is* a compliment,' said Melanie. 'Now I must go and do the lunch. You will stay, Bodger?'

'I'd love to.'

'It's cottage pie.'

Poggles groaned.

'Poggles,' said The Bodger, 'can anybody become a trainer?'

'Anyone who's not a disqualified person and who holds a licence from the Jockey Club. A woman can't hold a licence to train.'

'Why not?'

'Because the Jockey Club say not.'

'You keep saying "Because the Jockey Club say not." Do they have the final say?'

'Always and about everything to do with racing. They rule racing with a rod of absolute iron.'

'That's a pretty feudal system, isn't it?'

'Yes, but it's not such a bad system, when you come to examine how it works. The Jockey Club are answerable to nobody, which means they can bar somebody if they want to, without giving a reason. They nearly always do give a reason but they don't have to if they don't want to. That has its advantages. How often can you remember times in the Navy, or in legal cases come to that, where a bloke knows he's guilty, you know he's guilty, everyone knows he's guilty but you can't nail him because he's been charged wrongly, or there's a loophole in the law or there's some stupid reason why you can't get him. The Jockey Club don't have to worry about that. They can just say "We're awfully sorry, we believe every word you say, but we still don't want you," and that's that. There's nothing anybody can do about it.'

'But if they have no *legal* standing . . .'

'Ah, but it's much more cunning than that. They may have no legal authority but they have a terrific *moral* authority. You see, they own Newmarket Heath and if they warn you off Newmarket Heath then every other racecourse in the country will follow suit. You'll find you won't be able to attend a race meeting anywhere in the country nor have anything to do with racing in any capacity whatsoever. Not only that, the Jockey Club have gentlemen's agreements with almost every other Jockey Club abroad and you won't be able to get a job in Ireland or America or Australia or anywhere where there's proper racing. If a racing man's disqualified it virtually means the end of everything until he's reinstated. He can't go to a racecourse, he can't ride, he can't train, he can't do anything.'

'Suppose you started your own racecourse in opposition.'

'All right. Start your own race meeting. Just supposing you could afford it. No horse that ran in that meeting could run under the Rules of Racing again. Everyone at that meeting, every jockey, every trainer, every owner, every bookie, every stable lad, your judge, your vet, your handicapper, your clerk of the scales, your starter, your clerk of the course, your stewards, even the men who took the money at the gate and the men who parked the cars, *anybody* who had anything to do with that race meeting would be disqualified. I'm not even sure the Jockey Club wouldn't disqualify the Mayor and Corporation of the nearest town as well!'

'Name of a name,' said The Bodger, 'that's pretty sweeping!'

'It has to be. Everyone knows that racing is not exactly renowned for its honesty. There're some pretty sharp characters about and I can assure you, whatever its faults, the whole thing would be one hell of a lot worse without the Jockey Club.'

II

The Bodger had been thoroughly seduced by the Sport of Kings. Having never fallen before, he now fell all the harder. His so-called 'short acquaint course' in racing imperceptibly lengthened and broadened until it became an absorbed interest in all matters to do with the training and riding of racehorses. The Bodger began to manufacture excuses to go to Newbury and see Poggles. Poggles, though a busy man, still retained his naval officer's enthusiasm for talking shop, all night if need be, and The Bodger spent many instructive hours in Poggles' little office watching him do his homework and discussing horses and races, while mine host Isinglass looked after their glasses.

'What made you become a trainer, Poggles?' The Bodger asked, one evening. 'It's an unusual sort of job for a bloke to do when he comes out of the Navy.'

'If my old man had had his way, I would never have joined the Navy at all,' Poggles said. 'He wanted me to go in the army and then follow him here. It nearly broke his heart when I joined the Navy. However, all's well now. M'father started the stable when he came out of the army after the first war. He had a couple of good steeplechasers and he used to train them himself and win a few races with them. Various friends asked him if he would like to train their horses as well. This is quite a horsey neighbourhood, you know. My old man seemed to do quite well so he branched out a bit. He and my mother went to Newmarket one day and came back with two yearlings which they were going to race on the flat. One of them wasn't much cop, but the other, called Diocletian, by Hurry On, was a scorching good racehorse. He won seventeen races including the Newbury Spring Cup twice and he more or less put my father on the map. My father slowly built the stable up to what it is now, with between twenty and thirty horses in training, on the average. He never had a Classic winner, unfortunately, but he came damn close to it several times. The great thing about my old man was that he knew how to place his horses. He didn't have many horses but they did win races. Have you ever thought how a horse is entered for a race, Bodger? You don't just read the morning paper, see there's a race meeting on, open a fresh tin of horses, drive to the course and say to the Stewards "All right if I run my horse in the fifth race?" '

'I must admit, that's not so much of an exaggeration as far as I'm concerned,' The Bodger admitted. 'It's never occurred to me to wonder how a horse comes to run in one particular race rather than another.'

'I'll show you.'

Poggles pulled out a thick newspaper from under a pile of papers on his desk. The news items in the paper appeared to consist of closely-spaced paragraphs in fine lettering, printed on parchment-yellow paper which had a characteristic crackle.

'First of all, you need this. The trainer's guide, comforter and friend. *The Racing Calendar*. Costs five bob a week, published by Weatherbys for the Jockey Club, and it comes out every Thursday. It fulfils the same functions in racing as AFOs do in the Navy. It tells you all about the races, their conditions of entry, what weights the horses are carrying, who's been scratched, registrations of racing colours, partnerships, suspensions, anything you care to think of, all here.'

'But how do you go about entering a horse?'

'Just coming to that.' Poggles paused, while Isinglass did his work. 'Help yourself, Bodger. First, you look in the *Calendar* in the section marked Races to Close. You pick out a likely-looking race. Or races. You'll probably enter the same horse for several races near the same date or even in the same meeting. You can always scratch a horse but you can't enter him once the list has closed. This is where you often get arguments with the meaner type of owner; they don't want to pay the forfeits if their horse is not going to run. Having decided which horses in your stable are going in which races you fill 'em all in on this yellow form here.'

Poggles held up a slim yellow-papered book on which The Bodger could read the title: Nomination Form for Flat Races.

'Remember, you may have to do this weeks, months or even years ahead. Next year's Derby, for instance, closed a year ago now. Some horses used to be entered for Produce races before they were even born. But most minor races close roughly six weeks or so beforehand. If your chosen race is a handicap, and let's say for the sake of argument it is a handicap, the next important thing is the list of weights. You look at the *Calendar* when the weights for that race are published, see how much weight the handicapper has given your horse and say to yourself "'Cor send me old Aunt Fanny to fetch the beer, that handicapper needs his head looked at!" You want to scratch the horse. This time you use this white form.'

Poggles held it up: Declaration of Forfeit For Flat Races *Only*.

'You write in the name of the horse and the weight in handicaps, or the name of the horse and the owner in other races, and send it off. You've now scratched the horse and there's no harm done. Then when you look at the list of final acceptors in the *Calendar* you'll find that every other horse which might have beaten yours has also been scratched and if you hadn't been such a nit you'd have had the race in your pocket. Still, that's the way it goes.'

'*Now* . . .' Poggles returned his glass to Isinglass. 'This is thirsty work. Am I boring you, Bodger?'

'No, no,' protested The Bodger. 'This is a new world to me.'

'Right. *Now*, supposing you have a sudden rush of blood to the head and you've decided to leave the horse *in*. The horse will appear towards the front of the *Calendar* this time, under the heading Programmes of Meetings. But you've still got another chance to repent of your folly. There's this purple form. Forms For Late Declarations Of Forfeit And Declarations Of Runners. This is the famous Three-Day Forfeit Rule. This is the crucial one, the crossing of the Rubicon. In it you declare whether the horse is going to run or not. You can detach individual pages of this one (the yellow one and the white one have got to be sent in complete, by the way) and the pages must be in three days before the race. O.K., the race is less than three days away, the owner is on the telephone every hour on the hour, the press ring you up to check whether the horse has got four legs, and you're all set. Even *now*, you've still got one more chance to come to your senses. You can still write or telephone and scratch the horse any time up to eleven o'clock in the morning on the day before the race. This is the even more famous Overnight Declaration. This really *is* the Rubicon. When they say eleven, they mean eleven. After one minute past eleven, the horse *must* run, even though you've got to carry it down to the post on your back, or you incur a fine of not less than twenty-five pounds.'

Poggles nervously drained his glass, quite carried away by his own narrative.

'Race day comes, the horse has eaten up, kicked his stable lad through the roof, and done thirty quids' worth of damage to the horse-box. He's fit, he's possibly fancied, and you've bribed a jockey to ride him. The owner tells all his friends to back it and turns up with his wife and his Lebanese binoculars, all ready to cheer his investment home. The horse goes past the stands looking as if the whole thing was a mere formality. They're under starter's orders. They're off. They're running. Your horse is going well, nicely tucked in behind the last horse. It's a thrilling race, you don't know whether he's going to finish eighth or ninth. He finishes tenth, out of fourteen runners. Afterwards, the jockey tells you that next time you want him to ride a water-buffalo to let him know beforehand and he'll ride accordingly. The owner's wife turns to hubby and says "Darling, they tell me Noel Murless is a good trainer." You meet the handicapper in the bar sinking his fat chuckle-headed face in a can of ale and you cut him dead.'

Poggles regarded the bottom of his glass morosely. 'I don't know why you're laughing, Bodger,' he said, severely. 'This is a hell's serious business.'

'Oh I'm sure it is, Poggles,' chuckled The Bodger. 'But the way you spoke, it was obvious every word came straight from the heart.'

'It did, Bodger, it did.'

While Poggles wrestled with paperwork, acquired new owners and attempted to keep them contented, Josh, the head lad, was responsible for the day-to-day handling of the horses. Poggles himself had very little time to attend to the minutiæ of stable life; it was Josh who ran the daily stable routine, kept a sharp eye on the stable lads and the apprentices, and looked after the idiosyncrasies of every horse in the stable. Also, it was Josh's duty to stay and look after the stable while Poggles and Davey, the travelling head lad, were away at race meetings.

Josh had spent more than forty years in racing stables. He was the son of a Yorkshire miner and he had started work as a lad of ten, employed to carry food and water and to brush out the yard, being apprenticed as a jockey when he was fourteen years old and weighed five stones. He was a jockey of above average skill and success and had had several Derby rides on northern-trained horses. He might have set up as a trainer on his own but had never gained quite a wide enough reputation nor retained quite enough of his earnings to attempt it and so, at the age of forty, wearied by years of wasting, he retired as a jockey and became head lad, first to Poggles' father, and then to Poggles himself.

As head lad, Josh ruled the stable like a despot. He knew stable lads better than they knew themselves. No lad could make up an excuse which Josh had not used himself nor think of a dodge for avoiding work which Josh had not practised long before any of them were born. The stable lads and the apprentices very soon learned that they had to get up very early in the morning indeed to catch Josh napping.

Since The Bodger's Paul Revere act on the mare Elsie, Josh had mellowed towards him and looked upon him with a kindly, almost fatherly, eye and treated him as a nearer approximation to a human being than the normal run of racehorse owner. Josh initiated The Bodger into a rich racing mythology, handed down from generation to generation, which now found a worthy bard in Josh. The Bodger heard the legends of The Tetrarch, the Spotted

Wonder, the fastest racehorse ever to run on the English Turf, whom Josh himself had seen as a lad winning the Champagne Stakes at Doncaster. There were legends of other, apocryphal, horses (ridden by Josh) which were so slow that Josh had time to mark the punter's cards on the way up to the winning post. Josh related stories of the lonely Classic filly who was fretting herself to death in her box until a white goat was put in with her for company, and of the selling plater who one day ran so much above his previous form that the Stewards intimated that they wished to discuss the phenomenon with the trainer, for whom matters might have gone awkwardly had it not been discovered that the horse had been stung by a wasp as the tapes went up. The Turf had its sadder and darker side: Josh told of the savage stud stallion Vatican who decapitated and disembowelled the donkey given to him as a companion and who lived in filth because no lad dared go near him. Josh described how the horse was at last chloroformed and his eyes burnt out but the animal's screams were so terrible when the effects of the chloroform wore off that he was finally destroyed and died in appalling agonies. There were tales of triumph and disaster. Josh's grandfather had been present at Doncaster for the Cup when the drunken jockey Marlow, on The Flying Dutchman, flatly disobeyed Lord Eglinton's instructions and lost the race to Voltigeur. 'My grampa backed Voltigeur,' said Josh. 'He were drunk for a day and a night afterward.'

Josh spoke with that unique impediment of speech endemic in racing stables, which sounded as though it were due half to an adenoidal affliction and half to a wad of hay stuffed in each cheek. The Bodger had to listen hard to follow what was being said but once he had accustomed himself to the dialect, he was richly rewarded.

'Take this one, sir,' said Josh, opening the door of August Hill's box. 'It's a funny thing. You've heard of leavers, sir. Horses't won't eat up?'

'Yes,' said The Bodger.

'This lad's t'opposite. Proper glutton. Eat anything, he will. He'll eat yer boots if you stand about too long. That's why we put peat moss down instead of proper bedding.'

'I wondered about that.'

'If we put straw down, come back in t'morning, it'd all be gone. He'd eat it.'

'He's running at Manchester, isn't he?'

'Aye, if t'goin's mucky, I should have a bob or two on him, sir.'

In the next box was a flashy-looking two-year-old chestnut filly with four white socks, a white star, and streaks of yellow in her mane and tail. She had a long slender neck and nervous ears, and she watched Josh warily as he moved into her box.

'Whoah Susie. Whoah gal. This is Black Eyed Susan, sir. Funny thing, she'll only eat hay if it's on t'ground. She won't eat from manger. She's a lovely gel, but she's no heart for racing. She were badly left in her first race and the lad chased after t'rest of field and since then she's never done nothing. There's something funny with her.'

Next was a big, solid, brown horse. He stood with his legs slightly apart and started at The Bodger as though daring him to make his move.

'Semper Fidelis, his name is, sir.'

'Has he won any races?'

'He's won a couple. Nothing very smart. There's a funny thing. He came here from Newmarket and when he first come he wouldn't go anywheres by 'isself. Go anywhere in a string. Yer could've led him over a cliff if he were in a string but he wouldn't move out of this yard on his own. Kicked up hell, he did, the first time we tried taking him on his own. Threw the lad across t'yard, tried to take a bite out o'me. Proper acting up.'

'Is he all right now?'

'Oh yes, he's all right now. Like a lamb. It were just what he were used to, that's all.'

Next was Battlewagon. As always, he was friendly and anxious to be sociable. The Bodger had already grown enormously fond of the horse and was willing to be charitable about his contrariness on the racecourse. Josh, however, saw Battlewagon through less prejudiced eyes.

'There's funniest horse in t'yard. The way he went after that filly he looked a world beater. You were there, sir. You saw. Every time she made her move, he followed her. That takes a good horse. *Why* don't he do it on the racecourse, that's what I ask? At home he looks he could win the Derby not even breathin' hard. On the course, a donkey could beat him. It's a funny thing.'

It seemed that there was 'a funny thing' about every horse in the stable. The Bodger met Maiden's Prayer, who could not abide the rattling of metal and had to have his feed and water in plastic bowls; Parable, who could only be ridden by his own stable lad; Man Trap, who became uncontrollable at the sight of a dog; Ugly Duckling, who would run like a champion for six furlongs and literally walk every yard of any distance further; and Apollyon, who loved to look at his own reflection in a pond.

'I reckon you have to be something of a horse psychiatrist as well as a trainer,' The Bodger said to Poggles. 'You seem to have a stable full of neurotics.'

'Dead right,' said Poggles. 'But when you look at it from the most fundamental point of view, racing is an unnatural

147

thing to ask of a horse. After all, a two-year-old horse is still only a baby. Strictly speaking, he should still be romping about having the time of his life. Instead, he's broken early, subjected to the roar of the racecourse and made to work damned hard for his living. It's no wonder some of them become juvenile delinquents. Mind you, some of them love racing. Our wonder-horse for example. He gollops up his food, laps up his glass of milk stout like a Chief Stoker, and he really seems to enjoy race meetings. The trouble is that he seems to enjoy watching the others race. He acts like the reincarnation of a race commentator. I wish he'd act like a racehorse instead. Why, has old Josh been pounding your ears, Bodger?'

'He has, but I don't mind. I find him absolutely fascinating.'

'You should hear him on the subject of owners.'

Josh had indeed some strong opinions on racehorse owners.

'They come 'ere,' he told The Bodger, 'and say to me "Josh, 'ow's me 'orse?" and I say "Well enough, sir, in t'circumstances" and they go a mite green and say "*What* circumstances?". I say "I think your 'orse has a warm leg, sir, I felt it last night and it was a mite warm. It's all right now but I'm keepin' me eye on it". Then they carry on and shout and act like their dearly beloved son was dying of an incurable disease. If I told 'em one of the lads had a broken leg they'd say "The *horse* is all right though, ain't it?" They'll pay anything for the horses but they won't lift a finger for the lads. Look here, sir,' Josh turned and faced The Bodger squarely, 'If you paid ten grand for a racehorse, wouldn't yer want to know who looked after it? A lad can feel out o'sorts in t'morning and get mad with the horse and give him one just for sake of it. That upsets the horse.

148

The owner don't know nothing about that. But *Ah* know. *This* is where t'work's done. Jockey's only up on horse ten minutes on a racecourse. We have him the rest of time.'

'He's a bit prejudiced, of course,' said Poggles, when The Bodger mentioned Josh's opinions. 'But there's a lot of truth in what he says. Josh pretends to treat the stable lads like dirt but he's really got their interests at heart.'

'What does a stable lad earn?'

'Roughly three pounds a week and his keep. It varies.'

'It doesn't seem much.'

'They get tips when their horse wins, and they have other sources of income,' said Poggles cynically. 'Even when his horse hasn't won recently you sometimes see a lad blossoming out in a brand new coat or something. Ask him how he paid for it and he'll tell you he's just had a big bet. But he doesn't fool me, or Josh. We know he's been giving stable information to someone. Josh is an expert on stable lads. I always send them along to him before I take them on. He's got a theory that stable lads grow to their hands and feet, like puppies grow to their paws. If a lad's got big hands and feet he'll grow into a big lad.'

'Is that true?'

'Sometimes. It's a good theory, anyway.'

'Racing seems to be full of theories which don't always work out.'

Poggles laughed. 'There you've summed up horse racing exactly, Bodger.'

'Weren't you saying something about breeding being a matter of theories which don't quite work out?'

'Breeding is certainly an inexact science,' said Poggles. 'It sometimes works out, mind you. You get certain families from one particular stallion who are good over a mile and not a yard further, like their sire. You might have a stallion who was temperamental at the gate passing on his temperament to his offspring. Zucchero, for example. A friend of mine showed me a foal once which had a badly weeping right eye. I immediately thought there was something wrong with it but then he showed me its dam and her right eye was weeping, too. In theory, you ought to be able to juggle with X and Y chromosomes, and difference in parental ages, and Mendelian heredity principles and all that and produce the ideal racehorse for a given distance, but in practice it doesn't happen.'

'But how did it all start?'

'Oh I don't want to go into all that, Bodger.'

'Just a brief outline, Poggles,' pleaded The Bodger. 'Particularly about Battlewagon's breeding.'

'Well, it all started when some bright fellow in the seventeenth century crossed a native English breed with an Arab stallion. The pedigrees dating from that time are a bit hazy but three horses, the Darley Arabian, the Byerley Turk, and the Godolphin Arabian, seem to have been dominant. The whole system eventually shook down to three stallions, Eclipse, Herod and Matchem, and all racehorses today are descended from them. Take Battlewagon. On his dam's side he goes through Hyperion, Gainsborough, Bayardo, Bay Ronald, Hampton, Lord Clifden, Touchstone, Whalebone, Waxy, Pot8os, right back to Eclipse. On his sire's side, he takes his line through Airborne, Precipitation, Hurry On, Marco, West Australian, Melbourne, Comus and so on right back to Matchem. He's got any number of Derby winners in his background, if it's any comfort to you.'

'Good God,' said The Bodger, much impressed. 'He's better bred than I am!'

'The dam's side of racehorses is a bit more complex. Some

industrious character once worked it out that there were about forty tap-root mares and he listed them all by families. Battlewagon comes through Hyperion who goes back to a mare known as Old Bald Peg who's the sort of matriarch of family number six. But, as I say, you get some odd things happening. August Hill is a perfect case. Neither his sire nor his dam were any good at all on the racecourse and yet he's a cracking good horse. Even there, I expect if I cared to check it up I'd find that his grand-dam or his great-grand-dam won several races.'

The Bodger was sufficiently impressed by Poggles's opinion of August Hill to invest a speculative pound each way on him in the Manchester November Handicap. He was rewarded by the result in the evening papers. The race had evidently been run in Wagnerian conditions with thunderstorms overhead, a dark sky, and sheets of rain sweeping the course. The paper had a picture of August Hill being ridden home by a mud-drenched Tommy Sparling at 28–1. The Bodger rang up the next morning to congratulate Poggles.

'I'm afraid Peter's out,' said Melanie, who answered the telephone. 'But I'll pass on your message. How much did you have on him?'

'A pound each way.'

'That's another thirty-five pounds, Bodger! You *must* be lucky. Perhaps Battlewagon will have a chance in the Derby after all!'

12

The main event of the winter season, so far as naval public relations were concerned, was Navy Schools Week. The idea of a special recruiting drive directed at boys still at school had been conceived with great enthusiasm by Jimmy Forster-Jones (possibly because he was well aware that he would not be present himself to put it into effect), but it was one of which The Bodger heartily approved.

'You've got to catch them young,' he said to George Dewberry. 'It's no good waiting until they've grown up and then asking them to join the Navy. They've got more sense by then. You've got to get them young before they know what they're doing. What was it the Jesuits used to say? Give a boy to us until he's seven years old and anyone can have him after that. I'm not suggesting that we should recruit boys for the Navy at the age of seven but the principle is good.'

'I'm glad you feel that way about it, sir,' said George Dewberry. 'Because Jimmy arranged to give lectures on the Navy to several schools . . .'

'*What!*'

'. . . It was going to be his own contribution to Navy Schools Week, sir.'

'That slimy rattlesnake! He knew *he* wouldn't be here to do it!'

'Shall I cancel them, sir?'

'Good heavens no, you'd better not do that! They'll probably all rush off and join the RAF! We want to save them from that if we can! I suppose I'd better do it. But under protest, and I'm looking forward to the time when I meet Master James Forster-Jones again!'

'I'll confirm them then, sir?'

'Yes, you'd better. Not that they'll do any good,' said The Bodger sadly. 'You can convince a boy of anything. It's the *masters* we ought to be brainwashing. What are you doing for Navy Schools Week, George?'

'I'm in charge of the Navy exhibit at the Schoolboys' Exhibition, sir.'

'And the best of British luck to you, too!'

Navy Schools Week had also attracted the attention of those in the very highest quarters.

'I have great hopes of this scheme, Badger,' said Admiral Gilpin. 'Not from the publicity point of view, you know my views on that, but because the Sea Lords have been saying for years that the Navy hasn't had the right sort of officer recruiting since we gave up training in sail. Now's our chance to prove them wrong.'

'Yes, sir.'

'How is Blue Riband getting on?'

'We're going through a period of consolidation at the moment, sir. We should see more activity in March, sir.'

'I'm disappointed in Blue Riband, Badger. I had hoped for more results for the expense.'

'I agree, sir,' said The Bodger, sincerely.

'Keep me informed, Badger.'

'Aye aye, sir.'

The Bodger took his lectures to the schools very seriously. Conscious that his words might alter the whole course of several young lives, he searched for telling phrases to describe all that could possibly be said in favour of the Navy. He wanted to appear enthusiastic without being evangelical, winning without being over-powering, and persuasive without being prejudiced. It was a tricky problem.

'Why are you looking so worried, darling?' Julia asked.

'I'm trying to think what to say to these schoolboys.'

'Can't you just say to them what you used to say to your cadets?'

'Can't do *that!* It didn't matter what I said to the cadets. They were already *in*. These little horrors are not. They've got to be wooed, if that's the word. Trouble is, when I really get down to it, I can't think of a single reason why anyone should want to join the Navy nowadays.'

Before he went to give his first lecture, The Bodger called at the Schoolboys' Exhibition to see how George Dewberry was taking the strain. He found him, in uniform, standing forlornly with Angus MacBeetle, the Sea Cadet Liaison Officer, on a deserted platform. Schoolboys thronged the gangways but avoided the Royal Navy exhibit as though it were a head-master.

'How's business, Angus?'

'Very slack, I'm afraid.'

'Yes, I can see that. George, I should tuck that hip-flask away if I were you. It might give the wrong impression.'

The Bodger surveyed the Navy stand. It had been designed on lines of almost monastic restraint. It was nothing more than a shallow alcove lined with posters by Bill Beetleson at his most unexciting. In the centre stood a small deal table on which someone had optimistically placed a pile of pamphlets.

'This isn't very inspiring, is it?'

'No sir,' said George Dewberry.

The Bodger looked over at the Army stand, directly opposite. The Army had planned their exhibit with rare imagination. They had dispensed with posters and crammed their space with gadgets, weapons, levers and triggers; the centre-piece was the complete turret of a tank which could be trained, the gun barrels elevated and lowered, and the entire mechanism made to work by the schoolboys inside it. A cine film provided a realistic background of countryside studded with likely targets – a line of running men, two or three lorries, a dug-out bristling with guns and a guided missile site. A satisfying crack of gunfire was provided by the soundtrack every time the firing circuits were completed. The exhibit was undoubtedly a success; a plump artillery major was endeavouring to regulate the clamouring school-boys into some form of a queue.

The plump artillery major looked over and caught The Bodger's eye. 'Sold any good ships lately?' he called, and grinned triumphantly.

The Bodger gritted his teeth. 'Can't we do any better than this, George? Haven't we got anything like that tank over there?'

'I seem to remember a thing the Fleet Air Arm boys thought up for one of their air shows, sir. It was a contraption which pretended you were landing an aircraft on the deck of a carrier. It had a sort of film and sound-track.'

'Where is it?'

'I don't know, sir. I think Pat FitzBeetle had it last.'

The Bodger ran to a telephone.

'Pat, have you got a gadget which makes you think you're driving an aircraft on the deck of a carrier?'

'You mean the Flight Deck Landing Simulator?'

'Have you still got it?'

'Yes, it's in the store here somewhere. Why?'

'How long would it take you to get it out and over here?'

'Let's see. There's not a great deal to it. I could have it fixed by this afternoon?'

'That's fine, Pat. Will you do that, as quickly as you can. And look Pat, you remember some of that Blue Riband material you brought back from the West Indies . . .'

Confident that his instructions to Pat FitzBeetle would wipe that grin from the plump major's face, The Bodger braced himself for his own part in Navy Schools Week.

The first school on The Bodger's itinerary was St Dominick's, one of the very oldest schools in the Headmasters Conference. Though never achieving the eminence of Eton or Harrow, or of St Paul's, Mill Hill or Dulwich, St Dominick's had nevertheless prospered through the centuries since its foundation, producing a steady flow of citizens for the city of London – merchants, bankers, lawyers, doctors and parsons, with here a bishop and there a judge, an actor or two, and at least one prominent politician every other generation. The Bodger, who had taken the trouble to look them up in the Public Schools Yearbook, saw that St Dominick's was one of the largest and most prosperous schools in London, having over 700 pupils each paying £350 a year in fees. The Headmaster was Dr Frederick Tirrwit, MA(Cantab) and the Senior History Master, who doubled as Careers Master, was a Mr Basil Harman, BA(Oxon).

The Bodger was met by Mr Harman who was a fussy, middle-aged man with sandy hair and an air of concern for The Bodger as though he imagined that The Bodger had only reached the school after weeks of arduous trekking with snow-shoes and dog-teams across the Antarctic.

'I'm so glad you could make it, Commander,' he said, effusively, as though thankful that he could now recall the search parties.

'I'm very glad to *be* here,' said The Bodger heartily.

'Did you have a good journey?'

'Very pleasant, thank you.'

'Would you like some coffee?'

'That would be very nice.'

Mr Harman led the way to the Common Room. As they walked down the school corridors, The Bodger re-experienced that memorable smell, an essence distilled of football boots, radiators, ink and trousers, which took him back to his own schooldays. The boys they passed looked at The Bodger with dispassionate politeness, as though he were merely the new chemistry master.

The Common Room was a long chamber with a high ceiling. It reminded The Bodger in some ways of the wardroom of a naval barracks. It was similarly furnished with a score of armchairs, a large fireplace, a coffee urn, pictures, a letter rack, newspapers laid out on a table and a smell of tobacco. But, though very similar in appearance, the Common Room had not the same atmosphere as a wardroom. A wardroom was a place of relaxation where the heads of departments and responsible officers of a complex organisation could take their ease among their peers; the Common Room had an air of tension. It was plainly a refuge only, an uneasy sanctuary where the lion-trainers could snatch a quick cigarette before returning to the cages.

'White or black?' said Mr Harman, hospitably.

'Black, please,' said The Bodger.

'Oh, I don't recommend that.'

'Why ever not?' exclaimed The Bodger, in surprise.

'The coffee here is bad enough, white. Black, it's unspeakable.'

'Very well, I'll have it white. Tell me, do you have many candidates for the Navy?'

Mr Harman looked uncomfortable. 'I'm afraid we don't have any.'

The Bodger shrugged offhandedly. 'Perhaps this is an unusually *pacific* sixth form you have this term?' he suggested.

'I don't think we've ever had a candidate for the Navy.'

'Oh.'

'We did once have a boy who wanted to go into the Army,' Mr Harman said eagerly, as though anxious to make amends.

'And did he?'

'No.'

'What happened?'

'The Headmaster talked to him.'

'I see. Well then, what do your boys do?'

'They mostly go to university and then they do whatever their fathers did.'

'That must make your job as Careers Master very much easier?'

'Oh, it does. It's very simple. I have a system, you see. To the first boy on the list I recommend Archaeology, to the second Biochemistry and to the third Cost Accounting. Down to the twenty-sixth boy, Zoology.'

'And if there are more than twenty-six boys?'

'Then I start all over again, with Archaeology.'

'So N is for the Navy?'

'Not exactly. N is normally for Neurology.'

'And do they take your advice?'

'Never,' said Mr Harman. 'Of course, you must understand that the Careers Master is only a very recent innovation here. We've only had one in the last thirty years, you know. The Head at that time went to a conference and came back with the idea. I happened to be the most junior master in those days so I was given the job.'

'That reminds me, hadn't I better meet the Headmaster?'

'I'm sorry, I should have mentioned it, the Head asked me to make his apologies. He's at a conference today.'

'Perhaps he'll return with the idea that Careers Masters are unnecessary?'

'I hope so,' said Mr Harman, wistfully.

The Bodger finished his coffee.

'Shall we go?' said Mr Harman.

'I'm ready,' said The Bodger.

'We've arranged for you to use the library. It's a little more friendly than the main lecture hall.'

'Thank you,' said The Bodger gratefully.

When they arrived, the library was full of boys in blazers who stood up when Mr Harman and The Bodger came in. The Bodger was impressed by the size of his audience. For a school which did not profess to provide the Navy with officers, St Dominick's was obviously doing its best by The Bodger.

'It's very good of them all to turn up like this,' he said, aside, to Mr Harman.

'It's compulsory,' hissed Mr Harman, dampingly.

While Mr Harman was making a short introductory speech, The Bodger studied his audience. These boys were plainly the sixth form, the prefects, the captains and kings of the school, and they looked to The Bodger a pretty hard-bitten lot.

His introduction over, Mr Harman and the Librarian seated themselves behind The Bodger, ranged around him and sitting on the edges of their chairs as though ready to prevent him from actual private harm. The Bodger faced his audience, who gazed stonily back at him.

'Gentlemen,' The Bodger began, 'I've been asked to give you a short talk on the Navy as a career. I'm sure you'll understand that it's difficult for me to appear unprejudiced about this because I've been in the Navy ever since I left school. But first let me say, right away, that if you're looking for a job where you can make lots of money, where you work regular hours, have a steady nine to four job and a nice comfortable undisturbed married life, then the Navy is not for you. Anyone who wants any of these things from life might as well leave now. Nothing I'm going to say will interest him.'

For a moment it seemed that there might be a mass exodus from the library. Mr Harman half-rose threateningly from his chair. The crisis passed.

Unperturbed, The Bodger went on: 'I think the best way of describing the Navy is as a vocation. Even at its most mundane levels it demands a certain amount of giving without counting the cost. It's certainly a lifetime occupation. It's no good joining it hoping that it will fit you for something else. Because it won't.'

It occurred to The Bodger that he had begun his address on a particularly chilling note.

'I'm sorry I seem to have started rather gloomily,' he said, 'but let me tell you some of the things the Navy *can* offer. It's a young man's service. The average age of the ship's company in my last command, which happened to be a submarine, was twenty-four, including myself. In one submarine I served in, towards the end of the war, the ship's company had an average age of nineteen. I was the First Lieutenant, just twenty, and apart from the Captain I was the oldest officer on board. So the Navy is not an old fogeys' service. You also have to be very fit – fit in mind, boys who are under the delusion that they're Lord Nelson don't normally do well in the Navy, and fit in body. You have to have two working examples of everything, two ears, two arms, two legs, two eyes and two . . .' The Bodger paused, feeling that he was about to go into unnecessary anatomical detail. 'We count them, I can assure you, so you can't get away with anything.'

'. . . Contrary to popular belief, it's not necessary to have a father who is or was in the Navy. My father was in the Navy and I can't say it's helped me very much. It may be an advantage in that you'll have a naval background and may perhaps know a bit more about the Navy when you start but in the final shake-up it won't make any difference at all . . .'

The Bodger had taken great pains in preparing his speech. Carefully, he stressed the points which he thought would appeal to an audience of schoolboys – the chance of early and worthwhile responsibility, constant and cheerful companionship, and the opportunity to travel to faraway and exotic parts of the world at public expense.

When he wound up, The Bodger congratulated himself that he had presented the Navy's advantages favourably, indeed almost hypocritically.

Question time, therefore, came to The Bodger as an unforeseen awakening from complacency. The first question demonstrated that The Bodger had apparently omitted those very aspects of the naval profession which most appealed to the sixth form at St Dominick's.

'. . . How long do you have to do before you get a pension, sir?'

'There's no set time,' said The Bodger, a little put off balance by this materialist attitude. 'It all depends on what sort of entry scheme or specialisation the officer concerned is serving in. But I could safely say that all officers would be entitled to some form of pension by the time they're forty.'

'That's a considerably lower age than the average in industry, sir,' said a lanky youth in the front row. He had a studious look, spectacles, and long hair; The Bodger guessed that he was probably Chairman of the Debating Society or perhaps President of the Ballet Appreciation Group. 'Does that mean that when you leave the Navy you're being compensated for the fact that you can't do anything else?'

'Not at all!' protested The Bodger indignantly. 'The Navy has an extremely large and efficient organisation for re-settling officers and men in civilian life. Nobody who leaves the Navy need be out of a job. There are any amount of ex-naval officers doing very well in industry and farming.' The Bodger had a feeling that he was somehow contradicting something he had said earlier. 'But look here,' he added, hurriedly, 'I don't want to stress this aspect of the Navy. Can we just leave it that the Navy is not a dead end?'

'. . . Is it true that your pay goes up every two years, sir?'

'It's *reviewed* every two years. It doesn't necessarily go up every two years. It depends on the cost of living.' The Bodger had been prepared for questions such as 'What's the grub like?', 'What does rum taste like?' and even 'Why did you give up flogging?' but this calculating approach appalled him.

'. . . Why do they pay marriage allowance in the Navy, sir?' It was the Debating Society apache again. 'Isn't that an admission that the basic pay is not enough to keep a wife on?'

'I suppose it is,' said The Bodger, wildly. 'I suppose it is. I never thought about it. Any more questions?'

A stream of questions soon illustrated that his audience knew far more about naval codes of pay and allowances, health benefits, family privileges, and pension rights, than did The Bodger. The Navy Vote questions were bad enough; worse followed.

'. . . Why did you join the Navy, sir?'

The questioner was a fair-haired lad with almost angelic good looks. He was Captain of the First Boxing VIII.

'I don't know,' said The Bodger. 'I only know I did and I've never regretted it.'

'. . . What's the function of the Navy nowadays, sir, please?'

'The function of the Navy today is the same as it's always been. It's to defend this country at sea, in the politest manner possible.'

The Bodger came to the end of the questions feeling as jaded as a Minister after answering questions in the House on a matter about which his Ministry had a guilty conscience.

'I'm afraid that didn't go very well,' he said to Mr Harman.

'I thought it went surprisingly well,' said Mr Harman. 'Much better than the RAF wing-commander we had a year ago. We had to smuggle him out afterwards, through the side door in the gym.'

With which consolation, The Bodger drove to the Schoolboys' Exhibition. He found George Dewberry and Angus MacBeetle exhausted. The Flight Deck Landing Simulator had been an astonishing success. The Exhibition had never experienced such an attraction. The queue had stretched round the hall and into the street. The staff of other stands had joined it. Even the plump artillery major had sheepishly waited for his turn. Having had their turn, most of the queue ran to the end to wait again for another visit.

'I must have a look at this,' said The Bodger.

'The film's getting frayed,' said Angus MacBeetle, 'but I think it'll last a few more times.'

The Bodger climbed into the pilot's seat, checked his gauges, and grasped the joystick. Angus MacBeetle started the film and The Bodger sat back to enjoy one of the finest combined strip-tease and blue films ever set to calypso music.

13

The new flat-racing season opened sensationally. A 66–1 outsider won the Lincolnshire Handicap and Poggles rang The Bodger about Battlewagon.

'Bodger! That horse of ours!'

'Is he well?'

'No, he's not! He's been got at!'

'You don't mean he's been nobbled?'

'That's precisely what I do mean! The vet says he can't find anything wrong but there's no doubt that horse is in a very bad way.'

'I'll be right down.'

One look at Poggles's distraught face as he stopped his car outside the yard told The Bodger that something terrible had happened to Battlewagon.

'What's the story, Poggles?'

'When Jimmy Bones went into Battlewagon's box this morning he found he hadn't eaten up. Now that's absolutely unprecedented. If there's one horse that eats everything you give him it's Battlewagon. Jimmy couldn't find anything obviously wrong with him, neither could Josh. I had a look myself and I couldn't see or feel anything. We got the vet and he said the horse was ailing. I could have told *him* that, but the fact remains that horse shows every sign of being got at.'

'Oh my golly.'

'It's so ridiculous. Who would want to nobble Battlewagon? It's not as though he was likely to win anything. If he was favourite for the Derby or something, I could understand it.'

'Can I have a look at him?'

'Of course.'

Jimmy Bones and Josh were standing by the door of Battlewagon's box, each looking like an attendant at a morgue. A setback to the stable's Derby hope, no matter how remote that hope might be, was a major stable disaster. Other stable lads crept about the yard, casting worried looks at Poggles. It was like a death in the family.

The Bodger's first thought when he saw Battlewagon was how well he had wintered. He had filled out, broadened in chest and quarter and had developed into a really magnificent-looking colt. But his good looks were spoiled by his air of listlessness. He was standing with his back to the door of the box, and his whole frame suggested that he was about to give up the ghost.

'Hullo boy,' The Bodger called softly. The Bodger was aware that his bedside manner left much to be desired but, after all, he had never attended a sick colt before.

Battlewagon's normal good manners had deserted him; he made no sign that he had heard The Bodger.

'Hullo, Billy boy. What's the matter, boy?'

Battlewagon wearily turned his head and looked at The Bodger. His expression said unmistakably 'Go and get your free air someplace else, Buster'. He faced the wall again. The Bodger was reminded of Gwladys in one of her awkward moods. The thought of Gwladys gave The Bodger an idea.

'Poggles, how many fillies have you got in the yard?'

'A dozen or so, and the mare Elsie.'

'Can you get them out?'

'Why of course, but . . .'

'Don't say a word, Poggles. I've got a theory.'

'Do you want them all?'

'Every one. Jimmy, will you turn Battlewagon round so that he can look out into the yard?'

While Jimmy Bones coaxed, cajoled and finally bullied Battlewagon into a position where he stood with glassy eyes and lack-lustre expression facing the yard, the other stable lads put head-collars on the fillies and led them out into the yard. Josh went to fetch Elsie.

'Now what do you want us to do, Bodger?'

'Just lead the fillies up and down where he can see them.'

Solemnly, the lads began to parade the fillies up and down outside Battlewagon's box. There was none of their usual chatter and laughing; they did not find the situation in the least amusing. The stable's Derby entry was sick; anything which might help him back to health was worth taking seriously.

The parade of feminine horse flesh very quickly had a magical effect upon Battlewagon. His eyes regained their sparkle, his mane quivered and he began to utter a series of penetrating Rabelaisian neighs. His greatest enthusiasm was reserved for Elsie, his neighing reaching positive transports of delight whenever she passed him.

'The lecherous old pasha,' said Poggles. 'Funny how he seems to like Elsie best.'

'No it's not,' said The Bodger. 'It's not funny at all. It shows he's got good taste. He's got no time for these flighty young things. He likes his women mature.'

'I guess you're right. We'd better give him some exercise now, before he reduces that loose box to rubble.'

'You'll have to get the females out of the way first or there might be an ugly scene.'

'That's a point.' Poggles looked at the transformed Battlewagon and shook his head. 'I take off my hat to you,

Bodger. That's certainly done the trick. Wait till I tell that no-good vet.'

'All done by kindness, Poggles.'

'May be. Well, now that you're here let's discuss the plan of campaign for this season and try and decide what races we're going to run our wonder horse in before the Derby. He's entered for most of the classic trial races. I take it we're still determined to go through with this Derby business?'

'Most decidedly yes. Who would fardels bear, to grunt and sweat under a weary life, but for the thought that one day your horse is going to win the Derby?'

'Hah,' said Poggles, non-committally.

After the short lull between the Lincolnshire Handicap and the opening of the Craven Meeting at Newmarket, the first eight weeks of the season were perhaps the most fascinating of all to a student of racing. It was the time of the Classic trials, when the reputations gained as two-year-olds the year before were confirmed or discredited. Many fast two-year-olds failed to train on, while several undistinguished horses proved that they had blossomed through the winter. The racing press made pious pilgrimages up, down, and across the country, from Brighton to York, and from Newmarket to Chester, by way of Epsom, Newbury, Thirsk, Kempton and Lingfield Park, ever driven onwards by the hope of recognising, and forecasting, the eventual Derby winner. For owners and trainers it was a time when the capabilities of their horses were exposed to the public eye, with the same question always present in their minds, whether to allow their horses to take their chance in the Derby or to cut their losses and scratch them.

'I'd like to kick off on a course where we haven't had some frightful debacle in the past,' said Poggles. 'With a horse like Battlewagon that doesn't leave us much scope. He's run miserably twice at Newmarket and he chucked his jockey off at Newbury. That cuts out the Craven Stakes, the Free Handicap and the Greenham. It looks to me very much like the Two Thousand Guineas Trial Stakes at Kempton – or Thirsk.'

'Where's Thirsk?' said The Bodger. 'It sounds like somewhere in Alaska.'

'It's in Yorkshire. You drive up the Great North Road for about two hundred miles and then turn hard a gilbert right. The Classic Trial Stakes is a fair test of what we want. It's run over a mile and it's almost flat but it does have a stiffish left-hand bend and there's normally quite a good field. Also, it's worth two thousand quid or more.'

'Thirsk it is, then,' said The Bodger.

The Bodger looked up Thirsk in the AA Handbook, filled up his petrol tank and told George Dewberry to hold the fort.

'I won't be in tomorrow, George. I shall be trying to find one to beat the favourite at Thirsk.'

'Where shall I say you are, sir, if anyone asks?'

'Say I'm at the Admiralty Clock and Chronometer Store, Thirsk.'

'Is there such a place, sir?'

'I should think it highly unlikely!'

The Bodger was very pleased with Thirsk, with its budding trees on the far side of the course, its toy-sized stand and its rumbling Yorkshire voices which made their owners sound like bank holiday comedians. The meeting began very promisingly. The Bodger had a substantial lunch (on the racecourse executive) and, backing his own judgment, put a small sum on a rather engaging little filly called Four Little Heels in the first race at 10–1, and gratefully raised his hat to her and her jockey as they passed the post winners by a length. Two more whiskies in the Owners' and Trainers' Bar, using bookmakers' money, and The Bodger was prepared to feel optimistic even about Battlewagon.

'I must say I like this little course,' he told Poggles.

'It's very convenient. You don't have to walk miles to see the horses and put your money on. At some courses, Epsom for instance, it's a three-day camel ride from the paddock to the stands.'

Breathing out fumes of bookmaker-endowed whisky, The Bodger took up his stand in the owners' enclosure. He could not prevent himself feeling a touch of vanity when he compared his own privileged position with that of the scrambling hordes in Tatts. Owners were the aristocracy on a racecourse.

'And so they bloody well ought to be,' The Bodger told himself. 'Considering the amount of money it costs them.'

The Classic Trial Stakes had cut up more than Poggles had expected and Battlewagon was opposed by only four other runners: Sepulchre and Magistrate, both Middle Park Stakes runners trained in the north; Tirnanoge, trained in Ireland; and a 1,000 Guineas entrant, Gladiola, who was also trained in the north of England.

Battlewagon, numbered one and drawn one, was slowly away and for the first three furlongs was last in the field which was led at a good gallop by Gladiola. To The Bodger's gradually rising excitement, Battlewagon was seen to be making up ground steadily on the outside round the bend and entering the straight, with three furlongs to run, he moved up to second. A furlong later, when Gladiola's jockey was showing signs of activity, Battlewagon took the lead and The Bodger experienced that glorious surge of adrenalin in the blood stream which comes to a racehorse owner when he observes his property in front within winning distance of the line. Just as The Bodger was drawing breath for a cheer which would echo as far as the Great North Road, Battlewagon appeared to shorten his stride, Sepulchre and Tirnanoge came on, there was a period while Battlewagon and Gladiola seemed to be marking time backwards, the others galloped by, and Battlewagon reached the winning post third to Sepulchre and Tirnanoge, beating Gladiola a neck.

To appear in the winners' enclosure, even in the space reserved for the third horse, was a heady sensation for The Bodger. Poggles, however, seemed displeased and was muttering to himself. He and Tommy Sparling exchanged meaning glances as Tommy passed on his way to scale.

'It's something even to be third,' said The Bodger happily, giving Battlewagon a pat. 'A quart of best Guinness for you tonight, me lad.'

'Third out of five!' barked Poggles. 'He should have *won* that!'

Seeing the look on Poggles' face, The Bodger sobered. 'What went wrong then, do you think?'

'Probably the shock of finding himself in the lead was too much for him! Heaven help us in the Guineas. If I promise to be a good boy, do you think he won't let us down too badly?' prayed Poggles.

Except for the increased distance and Julia's fresh hat, the 2,000 Guineas, run over the Rowley Mile at the Admiralty Underwater Weapons Research Establishment, Newmarket, was almost a repeat of the Middle Park Stakes. The same wind blew over the same faces, Chemotaxis sprinted clear from the distance to win, and Battlewagon finished equal last, level with his chummy horse, Lapsus Linguae.

The following day La Petite made short work of a field of eighteen in the 1,000 Guineas. Poggles' only encouragement was that Gladiola, whom Battlewagon had beaten a neck at Thirsk, was second.

'It may be he just don't like Newmarket,' said Poggles. 'It may be that long staring Rowley Mile puts him off. You get that occasionally with lazy horses. They like hills and bends. It gives them an interest. Anyway, we'll see at Chester. He'll get all the curves he wants there.'

There was an exceptionally strong field for the Chester Vase, run over $1\frac{1}{2}$ miles and 53 yards at the Joint Services Tactical School, Roodee, that tight little circuit, bounded by the river, the railway and the city wall, where a fast break at the start was vital and a horse which led with the wrong leg was doomed, and where the crowd was composed equally of hunting matrons and Irish priests (who clearly had their cards marked by some extra-terrestrial agency, for The Bodger saw them queueing with infuriating frequency at the '£1 Pay' tote windows). The field was so strong that even The Bodger was pessimistic as Battlewagon was led out in the first spattering drops of a coming storm.

The Bodger's pessimism was justified. Battlewagon broke well, ran well despite the heavy rain which fell during the race, was well placed at the final turn, had every chance and finished eighth to Brash of ten starters.

'Well, I wonder what went wrong then,' said The Bodger.

Poggles raised helpless hands to the impotent sky. 'Perhaps it was the rain! Perhaps it was the going! Perhaps he didn't like the colour of somebody's hat in the paddock! How the hell should I know! Look Bodger, I've got other horses to worry about, horses that sometimes win races. I'll give him one more chance and if he makes another exhibition of himself I'll give you my share in him for nothing. If you still want him to run in the Derby you'll have to get another trainer. I'm a patient man but enough's enough. That horse has put years on me. I'll give him just one more chance. There's the Brighton Derby Trial or the Lingfield one. Which will you have?'

'Which is best?'

'There's not much in it. Brighton has the advantage that it's very similar to Epsom, but I always seem to catch a streaming cold there.'

'All right, we'll say Lingfield then.'

But before the Lingfield Derby Trial, The Bodger took the opportunity to go up to York ('Say I'm going to the Admiralty Materials Laboratory, Knavesmire,' he told George Dewberry) to see La Petite run in the Musidora Stakes.

The Bodger liked everything about York, from the clean-cut functional design of the new stands to the milk-grey starter's hack. It was a balmy spring day and the wind which blew among the trees in the paddock carried a promise of summer. The county families of Yorkshire (who make the most knowledgeable racing crowd in the Kingdom, apart from the taxi-drivers at Alexandra Park) sat on the bar-stools provided round the parade ring and discussed the points of the horses.

'Now is the winter of our discontent made glorious summer by this sun of York,' said The Bodger (rather obviously) to Poggles, who had brought August Hill up for the Yorkshire Cup.

'It can get perishing cold here too, you know,' said Poggles.

The one jarring note of the meeting was struck during the first race when Four Little Heels, whom The Bodger remembered kindly from Thirsk and who was again carrying The Bodger's money, started at odds on and was beaten four lengths by an outsider, whereupon The Bodger was forced to endure the blood-chilling sound of the county families of Yorkshire baying a beaten favourite.

The Bodger was shocked when he saw La Petite. She was a tiny filly, a very dark grey, with a short neck, coarse heavy head, and lightly-framed quarters. The Bodger thought her one of the ugliest racehorses he had ever seen. If this was the paragon of the English Turf, then The Bodger felt that he had made a long journey for nothing.

The Musidora Stakes, as a race, was a disappointment. The presence of La Petite had frightened away most of the field and only three fillies came under the starter's orders. The Bodger refrained from betting (it was a very hardened punter indeed who took an option when the best price obtainable for La Petite was 28–1 *on*) and was consequently neither richer nor poorer for the experience when La Petite broke like a lashing cobra, gathered her legs underneath her and streaked for the line to win by ten lengths, her jockey sitting almost upright.

'That was a real racehorse you saw there,' said Poggles, sourly, of La Petite, after the Yorkshire Cup in which August Hill was soundly thrashed by a one-eyed, pin-fired, Hob-dayed ten-year-old brown horse called Heaviside Layer.

The Bodger drove thoughtfully south down the Great North Road. It was just as well that La Petite was not running in the Derby.

The Lingfield Derby Trial was the last of the recognised trials and by the eve of it the racing press had already made up their minds that the Derby was likely to be won by Chemotaxis. Their decision was reflected in the ante-post betting, where Chemotaxis was a clear favourite at 7–1, the nearest horses Brash, Sepulchre and Abernotherone (winner of the Blue Riband Trial Stakes at Epsom) being on offer at 12–1. Battlewagon was not quoted at all, though his partner in despair, Lapsus Linguae, was available at 200–1. In the hurly-burly of the classic trials, where almost every reputation save that of Chemotaxis fluctuated with the result of each race, the fact that La Petite was still entered for the Derby went unnoticed except by a few astute racing journalists, who reassured their readers that Sir Leonard Brotherhood was certain to keep his filly for the Oaks.

The news that Sir Leonard intended to declare La Petite a runner for the Derby therefore sent a seismic shock through the racing world.

The Bodger was indignant. 'But he can't *do* that! The Derby's for colts.'

'No, it's not,' said Poggles. 'It's for entire colts and fillies aged three years. He's perfectly entitled to run La Petite in the Derby. It's unusual, certainly, but it's quite legal. Sir Leonard's already won the Oaks a couple of times, in fact I think I'm right in saying he's won all the Classics except the Derby. He obviously thinks that La Petite is the best chance he's ever likely to have of winning the Derby, and the best of luck to him. It was pretty acute of somebody to enter her for it at all two years ago. What's more, the rest of the field will have to give her five pounds.'

'But that's not fair!'

'Maybe not, but that's the rules. Colts to carry nine stone and fillies to carry eight stone nine pounds. I doubt if there's a colt in Europe who can give La Petite five pounds and a beating over a mile and a half. Don't get all steamed up about it. Bodger. It may never concern us. It all depends on Lingfield.'

The Bodger drove Julia and George Dewberry down to Lingfield with an unaccountable feeling of foreboding. The weather was appropriate. Lovely Lingfield looked grey and depressed in drizzling rain. Dense clouds hung broodingly overhead, as though shrouding a tragedy.

The Bodger's forebodings were amply confirmed. Battlewagon was restless in the parade ring, headstrong going down to the start and unruly at the start itself. He took one look at the starting gate and refused to approach it again. Having exhausted the starter's patience, he was forced to start behind the others. From a poor start, Battlewagon ran like a rogue, dropped to last, briefly overhauled the field and for a moment looked as though he might make a showing but after a mile and a quarter faded again and finished amongst a huddle of horses.

'That does it,' snapped Poggles. 'If ever I saw a horse that's *not* going to win the Derby, that's it. We'll scratch him now. Do you agree, George?'

'Maybe we're racing him too often?'

'Nonsense. He's a racehorse. Let him race. It's not as though he's even taking anything out of himself. He's just not trying.'

'We can't run him now, that's for sure. It would be a waste of everybody's time and money.'

'What do you think, Julia?'

Julia, who had been looking for Battlewagon among the other horses like Elisabeth searching among the pilgrims for Tannhäuser, said: 'I agree with George. But it's such a pity. He's such a lovely horse.'

'How about you, Bodger?'

'Can't we just let him take his chance?'

'Bodger, how much proof do you want! He's had a fair race every time, he's had every chance, and he's done exactly Sweet Fanny Adams. At Thirsk he proved that he runs idly once he hits the front. The Guineas proved that he's only got one pace and it's not fast enough. Chester showed that he can't come round sharp corners and quicken away. And here today he proved that he doesn't stay more than a mile and a quarter. You *can't* run a horse like that in the Derby! You just *can't!* This may be a fascinating hobby to you but it's my *job!* I've got my professional reputation to think about! I don't want to get the reputation of being a trainer who runs dead meat in the Derby just because his owners want to see their colours at Epsom. Because that's all that horse is. Dead meat! Bodger, you're forcing me to be very rude . . .'

'All right, Poggles. I've got the message. Can you give me a little time to think it over?'

'But Bodger, there's nothing to *think* over . . .'

'Just give me the weekend will you?'

'Very well. I won't post the forfeit until I hear from you on Monday morning.'

14

In the event, the decision whether or not to run Battlewagon in the Derby was taken neither by The Bodger nor Poggles. The Bodger should have been put on his guard by the knowing look he was given by The Tatler and Bystander, but he missed its significance and consequently obeyed the summons from Admiral Gilpin with no forewarning of disaster.

'Badger, I'm not a betting man,' began the Admiral, 'but I do have a bet each year on the Derby.'

A chilly finger touched The Bodger's spine. 'Yes, sir?'

'I happened to have lunch with the Sixth Sea Lord at his club yesterday and afterwards it occurred to us to study the list of probable runners for the Derby. After some thought we picked on a horse named Battlewagon and we understood from the club hall porter that this horse had never showed any previous form and that he could obtain for us odds of a hundred to one against the horse. This seemed to Admiral Dogpit and me very generous and we both placed bets of five pounds to win and five pounds a place. Each way, I think, is the technical term.'

The Bodger swallowed the lump of coal tar which seemed to be obstructing his throat. 'Yes, sir?'

'On returning to the Ministry after lunch I happened to mention my wager to Mr Rodney Bethel, of the Plans Department, and discovered from him, quite by chance, that Operation Blue Riband, of which we had all had such high hopes, was nothing more nor less than the code-name given to the process of training this very horse to run in the Derby.'

The Bodger was temporarily baffled by the name Rodney Bethel; it was only after some moment's thought that he associated it with the Tatler and Bystander.

'Naturally, I required confirmation of this astonishing statement. On enquiring for you yesterday afternoon I was informed by your secretary that you were visiting the Royal Naval School of Cookery, Lingfield Park. I then looked at the racing page of my morning paper and noted that the horse Battlewagon, owned by Mrs R. B. Badger and trained by Commander P. Terry-Neames, was engaged to run that afternoon at Lingfield Park in a race known as the Lingfield Derby Trial. I considered that this evidence was conclusive proof.'

'I'm afraid it is, sir,' said The Bodger. There was no point in attempting to bluff the thing out; the cat was out of the bag and among the pigeons to no mean tune.

'I also noted in my evening paper that the horse did not win.'

'I'm afraid that's true as well, sir.'

'Which brings me to the point of this interview. Mr Bethel has been informed that should any hint of this affair escape into the press he will be immediately transferred to an appointment in the Christmas Islands, whether or not he is responsible for the leakage. That should serve to guarantee his discretion. That leaves only the problem of yourself. When I recalled the information you had given me in the past concerning periods of consolidation, calibration and partial repair trials, using carbohydrates as fuel, my first impulse was to deal with the matter very severely. However, Admiral Dogpit has prevailed upon me to take a more lenient view. He has pointed out in a somewhat mercenary fashion that he and I stand to gain six hundred and twenty-five pounds each from the success of Operation Blue Riband. This consideration carries absolutely no weight with me but he also pointed out that Operation Blue Riband, mistakenly or not, has provided the service with some extremely valuable and good publicity. We have therefore decided on a compromise. If Operation Blue Riband, as I suppose we must continue to call it, proves to be a failure then there will be a board of enquiry into its failure, almost certainly followed by a particularly unpleasant court martial. If, on the other hand, Operation Blue Riband is a complete success then the matter will almost certainly be dropped. Do I make myself clear?'

'Quite clear, sir.'

'Then that will be all. Admiral Dogpit and I will await the result of the next renewal of the Derby Stakes with more than usual interest.'

'Aye aye, sir.'

George Dewberry was pacing up and down the floor of The Bodger's office.

'What happened, sir?'

'The worst! Richard's found out about Battlewagon and Operation Blue Riband!'

'Oh my God.'

'What's more, he and Seamus have put a fiver each way on Battlewagon! Ante-post, too. Can you imagine it? Where were they brought up? I don't know much about racing, but even *I* know that backing ante-post is the surest way there is to a permanent bench seat on the Thames Embankment. I learnt that at me mother's *knee!* I don't expect anything better of Richard, but *Seamus* ought to have more sense . . .'

'But what did he *say*, sir?'

'He said that Battlewagon had better win the Derby, or else! Or words to that effect.'

George Dewberry groaned and wrung his hands.

'Let's get hold of that bolshie trainer of ours.'

When Melanie, impressed by the urgency in The Bodger's voice, had succeeded in dragging Poggles to the telephone, he seemed reluctant to discuss Battlewagon.

'Now what?'

'Poggles, about Battlewagon . . .'

'Don't tell me. Let me guess. You want him entered for the Grand National, is that it?'

'No, I want him entered for the Derby and believe me, he's *got* to win! *Got* to!'

'But . . .'

'But me no buts, Poggles. I'm not joking, I don't care if he's only got three legs, I don't care if you fill him up with tranquillisers, I don't care if you have to take him down to the start in a *wheelbarrow*, but he's got to get up there and he's got to win!'

'What's happened now, then?'

Poggles listened attentively to The Bodger's account of his interview with Admiral Gilpin.

'So that's how it is. Do you know what Battlewagon was quoted at last night, Bodger?'

'I know. A hundred to one.'

'Do you know when the last horse won the Derby at a hundred to one? 1913, when Aboyeur won it. Even then, it was only on an objection.'

'Then it's about time it happened again.'

'Yes, I suppose that's one way of looking at it.'

'That's the way we've got to look at it from now on, Poggles.'

'All right, I'll declare him a runner. But if you take my advice you'll start preparing your defence right now.'

As he put down the telephone The Bodger remembered

Bert Beattle, the statistician. Admiralty Archie might be able to throw a more cheerful light on Battlewagon's chances.

The Bodger found Bert Beattle crouched intently in front of Archie. The giant computer was hard at work.

'Have you started your Derby summary yet, Bert?'

'Just doing it now. Almost finished in fact.'

'What does Archie tip?'

'Well, now that La Petite is running there's only one horse in it. Archie got quite enthusiastic about her. She's got the most incredible Derby profile I've ever seen. Archie says she'll start at odds on and romp it.'

'Any others?'

'We rather like the look of Chemotaxis but there seems to be a small doubt that he'll stay a really fast-run mile and a half. He's by Court Martial and most of Court Martial's stock only just get a mile, let alone a mile and a half. Sepulchre, Tirnanoge and L'Arlesien are quite promising. Abernotherone looked good until he was scratched.'

'Is he scratched?'

'Scratched this morning. He got loose and cut himself on some wire rather badly. The best outsider is Lapsus Linguae.'

'Lapsus Linguae!' said The Bodger scornfully. 'That's a *useless* horse! I've seen him run myself.'

'Perhaps, but he's my each-way selection. Nobody seems to have noticed that he won an obscure mile and a half race at Salisbury three weeks ago, in a Derby-winning time. La Petite to win, Lapsus Linguae and Chemotaxis for places, those are our selections.'

'How about Battlewagon?'

'There's a peculiar thing. He's actually got a very promising Derby profile but there's something missing, as though the top of the graph had been left off. Are you sure you've told me everything you know about that horse?'

'Quite sure.'

'I just ask, because I've fed in the thirty-seven criteria and Archie still comes up with the Solution Reserved indication.'

'What does Solution Reserved mean?'

'Insufficient information. There's some factor still missing which Archie needs to complete the comparison. What odds are they offering against him?'

'Hundred to one.'

'You're being robbed. Archie puts his chance at precisely five hundred and twenty to one against.'

'Machines can be wrong,' retorted The Bodger, slightly nettled.

'Oh, quite. I've never claimed a hundred per cent accuracy or anything near it. I know where *my* money's going though, all the same.'

Depressed by Admiralty Archie's clinically realistic opinion of Battlewagon, The Bodger went back to his own office and sat watching the telephone, expecting it to ring at any minute. The Bodger knew that there would be at least one further development to Operation Blue Riband before the day was out.

The Bodger sat expectantly in his chair. The telephone remained quiet. The Bodger remembered that Jimmy Forster-Jones had recommended Tommy Spares, the barber, as a convenient hide-out when the office became too oppressive. The Bodger decided that he needed a haircut.

Tommy Spares was a barber of the old school who disdained more fashionable names, such as hairdresser or hair stylist, for his profession. His name and proper style, 'T. Spares, Barber' were uncompromisingly printed in gold lettering above his door, beneath the spiral red, white and blue coloured pole.

Tommy Spares' shop looked as if it had been constructed

at the same time, and by the same builder, as The Vaults. A glass chandelier hung from a dark, grimy ceiling. The walls were plastered with photographs of horses and jockeys, old calendars, and fly-specked advertisements for hair tonics. The three barbers' chairs, only one of which was actually in use, were made of heavy black wood with leather padding. The deep basins were of green and grey veined marble with shining brass taps. Tommy Spares used no electric cutters but worked entirely with long scissors and cut-throat razors. Tommy Spares himself was a thin, stooped man in a white overall. He paused in his work to look at The Bodger.

'Good morning, sir. Just take a seat sir, and I won't be long.'

The Bodger sat down on a long wooden bench. The literature provided for Tommy Spares's clientele to read while they were waiting was wholly about horse and greyhound racing and the clientele themselves looked as though they had stepped directly off a racecourse. They were talking about horse racing.

'She started at five to four on,' the man sitting next to The Bodger was saying. He was wearing a brown and black checked overcoat and a brown cloth cap and he looked like a bookie's clerk. 'She should have walked it. And what did she do? That jockey pulled her, it stands out a mile. It was obvious. Gravy Train should never have beaten her at those weights. Four Little 'Eels they call her. That's not what I call her.'

The Bodger pricked up his ears. They were talking about that nice little filly whom The Bodger had witnessed in triumph at Thirsk and in disgrace at York.

'Pulled her,' said the man in the checked overcoat. 'He should be warned off. And the trainer, too.'

'No he shouldn't,' said The Bodger.

The whole shop focused their attentions upon The Bodger.

'How do *you* know, mate?'

'Because I was there. She ran very well at Thirsk a few weeks before, I saw her do it, and that's why she started favourite at York. She was just given too much weight, that's all.'

Tommy Spares goggled at The Bodger as though The Bodger had suddenly grown another head.

'You a racing man, sir?' he said, incredulously.

'Not really,' said The Bodger, modestly. 'I just happened to have been there. Were you there?' he asked the man in the checked overcoat.

'Jim?' Tommy Spares exploded his breath in derision. 'He's never been on a racecourse in his life. He wouldn't know a horse if it got up and bit him. Armchair punter, that's our Jim.'

'You don't have to go there,' Jim said defensively. 'You can see just as much from the papers.'

'You keep quiet, Jim,' said Tommy Spares. 'This gentleman here knows what he's talking about. You've met a real punter now, Jim, so keep your mouth shut and show a bit of respect.'

The Bodger beamed at the unexpected compliment. He remembered a joke Poggles had told him. 'Talking of pulling horses,' he said airily, 'I remember about two years ago at Kempton as blatant a case of pulling as I've ever seen in my life. The horse should have won by ten lengths but it was beaten a short head.'

'I remember that,' said Jim. 'Horse called Giraffe's Toupee, wasn't it? Selling plater.'

'There happened to be a particularly young and keen

Steward there that day,' The Bodger went on, ignoring the interruption, 'and he said to one of the older Stewards "Did you *see* that? Did you see what I saw?" The old Steward said "Of course I saw it". So the young Steward said "Well, aren't you going to do anything about it?" And the old Steward said "Of course I'm doing something about it. I'm making a mental note to back it next time out!".'

The joke went down very well. The Bodger felt himself being accepted into the Club. He was delighted to discover that he could hold his own in racing circles; it was like discovering a new dimension in his conversation.

'Have you got anything for the Derby, sir?'

'Battlewagon,' said The Bodger unhesitatingly.

Tommy Spares dropped his scissors. The man in the chair craned his neck to look at The Bodger. Jim smothered a laugh.

'That's trained by Terry-Neames, isn't it, sir?' said Tommy Spares politely.

'That's right,' said The Bodger.

'He deserves a Derby winner,' said Jim. 'His old man never made it. I'd like to see the son do it. But he won't do it with that donkey. Trouble with Terry-Neames is he's got some terrible owners.'

'*Really?*' said The Bodger.

'Oh, shocking! Think they know best. Won't let him run the horses in the proper races. Try and tell him his business. Now that ain't right. If I had a racehorse I'd pick myself a good trainer and let him get on with it.'

'The day you get a racehorse, Jim,' said Tommy Spares, 'I'll give free haircuts to the whole o'London!'

'That'll be the day,' said the other customers.

The Bodger had lost all the ground he had gained. His mention of Battlewagon for the Derby had relegated him once more to the ranks of those who patently knew nothing about racing.

'If you feel like backing your fancy, sir,' said Tommy Spares, 'Tigger over there will take your bet for you and see it gets on.'

Tigger was a dwarf-sized man sitting in one corner who had taken no part in the general conversation. He was wearing a blue pinstripe suit and a shirt with no collar. He had a red scarf wound round his neck and a dark blue cloth cap. He was sitting under a notice which said No Betting Slips and he was plainly the resident bookies' runner.

'I shan't bother just now,' said The Bodger. 'I'll wait till I get to the course.'

'Just as you like, sir,' said Tommy Spares in a voice which implied that if The Bodger was set on losing his money it didn't matter much where he lost it.

Freshly cut and pomaded as to the head, The Bodger returned to his office more depressed than he had left it. Tommy Spares's clientele's opinion of Battlewagon, though left largely unexpressed, had been more condemning even than Admiralty Archie's.

The telephone was ringing. It was the call The Bodger had expected.

'Bodger,' said Jim Sewter, 'what's all this I hear about Operation Blue Riband?'

'What have you heard about Operation Blue Riband?'

'That it's all off because of the expense.'

'I don't know where you heard that but it's quite wrong. Blue Riband is very much still on. It's approaching its most critical stage.'

'Getting tense, eh?'

'Yes.'

'Oh well, I don't expect we'll use it but thanks very much all the same.'

'Sorry to disappoint you. I'll let you know in due course.'

Nevertheless, several enigmatical paragraphs about Operation Blue Riband appeared in the papers next day. The Bodger did not need much intelligence to appreciate that the press had their eye on Operation Blue Riband. One slight suspicion of failure and they would be round like jackals. The Bodger began to include petitions for the continued good health and welfare of one grey racehorse in his prayers.

15

Derby Day dawned clear and bright. By ten o'clock in the morning the temperature on the Downs was rising to seventy in the shade and by eleven o'clock most of the racegoers on the hill were already in shirt-sleeves. By noon, the police and the racecourse officials were agreeing that it looked like being a record crowd even for Derby Day. The fairgrounds in the centre of the course and on the hill behind the grand-stand had arrived the day before and were open for business. Traffic was accumulating as far away as the Kingston By-pass and the Brighton Road; lines of cars, vans, coaches, open-topped buses and caravans were creeping towards the course by every road. Everyone was on his way to Epsom Downs. Newmarket might be headquarters, Ascot might be Royal, Goodwood might be glorious, but Epsom had the Derby and it seemed that everybody in the British Isles who could get or take the day off was assembling on the Downs to see it.

The Bodger, who drove down with Julia, had never in all his experience seen anything like Epsom Downs on Derby Day. The sights, smells and sounds battered at their senses as they drove slowly in a line of traffic past hot-dog stands and ice-cream vans, a sign: 'Jellied Eels 2/6d', a helter-skelter painted in rose and gold, a line of gypsy caravans with neat curtains and flowers in brass trumpet-shaped vases ... 'The *Original* Gypsy Rose Lee!', 'Madame Petulengro', 'In *Direct* Touch With The Stars!', an orange-lettered sign: 'Hamburgers and Chips', the smell of onions and frying oil, the cry of a newspaper seller, hot chocolate, Guess Your Weight, sausages and mustard, horns hooting, the scuffling of tens of thousands of feet, 'The Mystic Queen', coconut shies, 3 Throws–6d, Ladies 4 Throws–6d. The crowd pressed forward, darting into the gaps in the traffic, the policemen gesticulated furiously . . . Silver and red and green and purple and white coaches from Clacton and Middlesbrough and Cardiff and Stafford and Aldershot swung giddily one by one into the car parks . . . red balloons for sale, blue and yellow umbrellas, silver horse-shoes, the drumming of fairground engines, a string of coloured bulbs, lucky white heather, Race Cards, lurid yellow lemonade, 'I gotta horse to beat the favourite!', a shooting gallery, shuffling feet, 'Christ Died to Save Us', a pyramid of dolls with china-blue eyes, Late Paper, 'You've got a lucky face, dear', the shadow of the grandstand, iron gates decorated with medallions of past Derby winners, Papyrus, Captain Cuttle, exhaust fumes, threshing gears, the smell of bitter beer, a hotter sun . . .

'This isn't a race meeting,' gasped The Bodger. 'It's absolute bedlam!'

'Isn't it heaven?' said Julia.

The Bodger twisted his neck uncomfortably. 'It might be if I hadn't got all this stupid morning dress nonsense on.'

'It isn't nonsense, darling. You look terrific.'

'It's all right for you. That dress only weighs about a pound. I'm carrying the full nine stone.'

The traffic had come to another halt. They had stopped beside a tipster who had already drawn a small crowd of mesmerised people. 'Jack The Namer' proclaimed the banner over his head, 'Tipster to the Crowned Heads of Europe! See Press and Jockey Club for Proof!'

'. . . When did I ever tell you a lie? *You* were here last

year! You sir, you were here last year! You heard me give the winner of the Derby! This is a five pound note! Two more seconds and it's fifty! *Fifty pounds* I'll give to the man who proves me a liar . . .'

The traffic moved on for a short distance. This time they stopped beside a man who despite the heat was wearing a heavy grey overcoat. The banner above his head read The Wages Of Sin Is Death.

'Shouldn't it be "The Wages Of Sin *Are* Death"?' said The Bodger.

'It doesn't matter, darling. Listen.'

The man in the overcoat had an indefatigable, bellowing voice which could rise above storm and tempest, fire and foe, and the crowd at Epsom on Derby Day.

'My friends, listen while I read to you from the Staff of Life . . .'

His audience, which consisted of four men also in grey overcoats and a young Indian in a blue turban who continually slapped a thick rolled newspaper against the palm of one hand, shifted their feet and looked at the ground.

'. . . Matthew, twenty-one, eighteen. And when He saw a fig tree in the way He came to it, and found nothing thereon, but leaves only and said unto it, let no fruit grow on thee for ever. And presently the fig tree withered away.' The man shut his Bible and looked up. 'Now there's an interesting story, my friends. When I was in the Army during the war my sergeant-major didn't like me. Many a time he stood in front of me and bawled me out something terrible. But did I shrivel up? Did I wither away and die? Did I? You see me standing here. Which just goes to prove that Jesus Christ knew some swear words my sergeant-major didn't even know . . .'

'Sporting paper, all the winners!'

A newspaper was thrust through the car window. The Bodger bought it and gave it to Julia.

'Who do they say will win the Derby?'

'La Petite. Must Be La Petite, it says.'

'Does it mention Battlewagon at all?'

'I don't think so ... Wait, here's a bit at the bottom. "Battlewagon. Placed once in eight races. No chance. Here's one wagon I won't be climbing on!".'

'*Cheeky* fellow!' said The Bodger, indignantly.

'I do hope George Dewberry will get here all right. I don't think we ought to have trusted him to come by himself. He's bound to have been drinking last night.'

'Well, God, if he can't make it in time to see his own horse run in the Derby that's his own look-out,' said The Bodger unsympathetically.

'He might be with Poggles and Melanie.'

But Poggles and Melanie had not seen George Dewberry all day.

'How's Battlewagon?' The Bodger asked Poggles, at once, while Julia and Melanie studied each other's hats.

'Oh, just the same as ever. Seems to think the Derby's been laid on for his benefit. I think he's got the idea the other horses are only here to make up the numbers so the punters can back each way!'

'How splendid! You seem a bit more cheerful than when I last saw you, Poggles?'

Poggles scratched his chin. 'I don't know, Bodger. There's *something* about that damned horse. I don't know what it is. Don't tell anyone, but I've got fifty quid on him.'

'Hells bells and buckets of blood!'

'I know,' said Poggles ruefully. 'I know I need my head examined but then I've needed my head examined all along in this business. I might as well go the whole hog now I've got this far. I thought you were bringing George Dewberry with you?'

'No, we haven't seen him at all,' Julia said anxiously.

'He'll turn up for the champagne at lunchtime,' said The Bodger.

'He'd better come soon,' said Poggles, 'or he'll find himself snarled up in the traffic. Let's just take a walk along the rails. I want to see how they're betting.'

The bookmakers in front of the grandstand were warming to their work with a sustained powerful chorus in response to the frantic conducting of the tic-tac men. It seemed to The Bodger that the roar of the ring was several decibels louder at Epsom than at any other meeting. The bookmakers were softening up an audience which had a large proportion of overseas visitors who, nurtured on totalisator-only courses at home, were gazing in wonder at their first sight of race-course bookies.

One bookmaker in particular had attracted a large crowd round his board. He was a giant of a bookmaker, the epitome of the Ring, a veritable Nebuchadnezzar among bookies. His gigantic frame was clothed in a dove-grey silk suit and topped by a pearly grey bowler, he had a large gardenia in his buttonhole and a voice like John the Baptist.

'. . . Keep me busy! Aye aye, keep me busy! I'm offering over the odds!' He snapped the roll of tickets in his hand with a tearing, rippling sound. 'Aye aye, don't disappoint me! I'm here for your benefit! Thank you, Madam, ten shillings each way, Epsomist? That's a pony to a half a win, six pound five to a half a place! Number one hundred and twenty-four, I thank you! Here you are, madam, I'll write it down on the back of the card for you. Thank you, sir, eighty pounds to five Royal Exchange. There you are, a brand new Rolls for a fiver! I'm looking for business! Aye aye, I'm looking at yer! You *can't* get these odds anywhere else, ladies and gentlemen! Thank *you*, sir. Two pounds to win, Solomon's Seal. That's one hundred pounds to two, Solomon's Seal. Look at that, a cruise round the Canary Islands and all for two quid! I'm not kidding . . .'

'The only person who'll be going on a cruise round the Canary Islands when this is all over will be him,' said a disillusioned voice in the crowd.

'Aye aye, I heard that! Keep me busy now, I'm offering over the odds . . .'

The betting market had already taken firm shape. La Petite was undisputed favourite at 6–4 on, with more money going on her every minute, but there was still plenty of money for Chemotaxis at 7–1. The other prices ranged from Tirnanoge and L'Arlesien at 12–1 to Lapsus Linguae at 100–1. The Bodger was surprised to see Battlewagon on offer at 50–1. Even as The Bodger watched, Battlewagon's odds were cut to 33–1.

'What's happening, Poggles? I thought he was at a hundred to one?'

'Sentimental money going on him, I expect. I shouldn't be surprised if half the Navy haven't gone mad and backed him. All the professional money's going on La Petite, you'll notice.'

'I'd better get my money on quick, then.'

The Bodger raced up and down the rails and found only one bookmaker still offering 50–1 against Battlewagon. It was none other than The Bodger's enemy from Newmarket.

'Twenty pounds to win, Battlewagon,' said The Bodger, in a tense voice. This was by far the biggest bet he had ever struck in his life.

'One grand to twenty pounds, Battlewagon,' said the

bookmaker emotionlessly, as he threw The Bodger's money into his bag.

'Aren't you going to put that away for your old age fund?' The Bodger asked.

'Nope. That's going towards m'daughter's education. She's head-girl at Roedean.'

'Oh,' said The Bodger, learning the truth of the old racing saying 'Never bandy words with a bookie under the shade of his own umbrella.' However, The Bodger had the satisfaction of seeing that the bookmaker immediately cut Battlewagon's odds to 33–1 and, a few minutes later, to 25–1.

'Robert darling, do look at the people over there,' said Julia.

'My Golly, yes!'

The Bodger had often heard the phrase 'a sea of faces' but Epsom Downs was the first time he had seen the phrase in fact. From Tattenham Corner across the Hill and down to the Downs Hotel the course was jammed with people. Every vantage point was taken and every face was turned towards the course. Looking through his binoculars The Bodger could recognise some familiar figures. There on the top of an open-topped bus on the other side of the course were the Sea Lords, from First to Sixth, with attendant staffs; the lower deck of their bus was dark and shadowy with stacked crates of beer. Almost next door was the Naval Public Relations Department bus. The Bodger could pick out Frank Bethell's flaming red beard, old Bill Beetleson's silver hair, Jake van der Beetle's white goatee and the swarthy, Iberian features of Beetle King of Arms. George de Beetle was wearing a very dashing black and white checked cloth cap, his only concession to the occasion; next to him sat Bert Beattle, bottle of beer in hand, confident of Admiralty Archie's powers and displaying the complacent smile of a man who knows his money is safely on the most scientifically probable horse at the best obtainable mathematical odds (though he had a saver on Battlewagon out of loyalty to The Bodger). On either side for some hundreds of yards were drawn up representative bus-loads from nearly every home-based ship and shore establishment in the Navy. All, by their appearance, had been, and still were, looking upon the ale when it was a very dark nut-brown colour indeed.

'I only hope the balloon doesn't go up somewhere this afternoon,' The Bodger said to Poggles. 'Looking at those buses over there, I would say that about seventy per cent of the Navy is here at Epsom.'

'Best of luck to 'em,' said Poggles. 'I can't think of anything else I'd rather be doing on an afternoon like this. I must go and get Battlewagon ready. I'll see you later. What are you doing about lunch?'

'I don't think either of us could manage any lunch. A sandwich is about all that we could eat right now.'

'I know just how you feel. I wonder what's happened to George?'

*　　　*　　　*

George Dewberry was just getting out of bed. His pre-Derby Cointreau and soda party had not broken up until five o'clock in the morning when George had slumped, fully-clothed, on his bed and slept like a dead man. His landlady had made several attempts to wake him but had finally abandoned him when it was time for her to start out for Epsom herself. George Dewberry had awoken at half past one in the afternoon but so bad were his muscular co-ordination and his judgment of distances that it was half past two before he had undressed himself, washed, shaved, found his morning suit, dressed again, and begun the drive to

Epsom. The runners were in the parade ring when George Dewberry reached the beginning of the Kingston Bypass and saw the stationary lines of cars stretching into the distance.

George Dewberry switched on his car radio. Plainly, it was going to be the nearest he was going to get to Epsom that afternoon.

'. . . Good afternoon to you from the roof of the grand-stand at Epsom on the most glorious afternoon for racing . . .'

The lines of cars began to move up, until George Dewberry could see the cause of the obstruction. The road was under repair on the crest of the next hill.

'. . . Well it's a brilliant scene down below me on the members' lawn, grey top hats and summer fashions, and away to my left the bustle of Tattersalls and then right across the course, as far as the eye can see, people, people, masses of people . . .'

The queue was edging forward, a few yards at a time. When the runners, riders and the draw were being read out, George Dewberry could just faintly hear the sound of the pneumatic drills.

'. . . A field of twenty-one. And here they are. First, number one, Mr F. C. Troup's Hard Bitten, ridden by Bobby Patch, drawn eight, and wearing blinkers and trained here at Epsom by Captain Tubby Turvil. Number two, Brigadier Tregonwell's Trefoil, ridden by Don Bryant, drawn fourteen and trained in Ireland by Charlie O'Higgins. Number three, Madame Leonie Tourbillon's L'Arlesien, ridden by Marcel DuPreix, drawn one and trained at Chantilly by Roger Croissant . . .'

The sun beat down upon the roof of George Dewberry's car. Giddy swells of nausea attacked him, from which he was rescued by the mention of a familiar name.

'. . . Number Seventeen, Mrs R. B. Badger's Battlewagon, ridden by Tommy Sparling, drawn ten, and trained at Newbury by Commander P. Terry-Neames. Number eighteen, Sir Leonard Brotherhood's La Petite, the favourite and the only filly in the race and in fact the first filly to run in the Derby for some years, ridden by Forres Stirling, the champion jockey, drawn five and trained at Newmarket by Ned Larkin . . .'

While the parade was in progress, George Dewberry travelled some five hundred yards. The noise of the drills rose in proportion from a slight irritation to a definite nuisance.

'. . . Then there's Battlewagon, a grey colt by Ship of the Line out of Sun of Austerlitz. He's actually related to La Petite, La Petite being by Ship of the Line out of that very fast Nearco mare Petite Beurre, but there I'm afraid the resemblance ends. He had the unenviable distinction of being unplaced in all his races as a two-year-old. He was actually placed in the Middle Park Stakes on the judge's error but the mistake was corrected, you'll remember, later that afternoon. He's not shown much form this season either. He was third of five to Sepulchre and Tirnanoge over a mile at Thirsk in April but he's run disappointingly since. He has the reputation of being a bit of a rogue and he may not be absolutely genuine. One can only say that it doesn't seem likely that he'll be concerned in the finish . . .'

'Bloody idiot!' grumbled George Dewberry. 'Stupid fellow, doesn't know what he's talking about!'

'. . . But I must say he looks very fit. He's a heavy-topped colt, but cool in his coat and looking a great credit to his trainer Peter Terry-Neames who took over the stable after the death of his father . . .'

'That's *better*,' said George Dewberry.

197

'. . . Then La Petite! Carrying the famous chocolate, green and pink colours of Sir Leonard Brotherhood. She's on her toes, not a good-looking filly, but her performances belie her looks. She's won eight races from eight starts in her racing career, including the Thousand Guineas. She's never been beaten and she's starting a very firm favourite today, the hottest favourite since Tudor Minstrel. I was talking to Sir Leonard this morning . . .'

By the time the horses had come under the starter's orders, George Dewberry was straining to hear above the periodic bursts of drilling but the effects microphone recording was so good that in his moments of clarity George Dewberry could even hear the urgent shouts of the jockeys, terrified they would be left at the post in the Derby. 'Not yet, sir! No-no-no-sir! Not yet, sir!'

'. . . Mr Alec Marsh, the senior Jockey Club starter, has mounted his rostrum. They're coming into line . . . But now Brash has turned round. And so has Tirnanoge. And Royal Exchange, and Battlewagon. Oh, now there's six or seven horses all turned round. Now here they are again, coming into line . . . and this time it's Solomon's Seal who won't go into line. And now Hard Bitten, and now Brash is lashing out and has turned right round. And here they come again . . . they're coming into line . . . it looks as if they'll go this time . . . and *they're off!* To a very good start, I should say, only Brash was rather left, by some six or seven lengths, and straightaway it's Solomon's Seal who's gone into an early lead, Solomon's Seal going on from L'Arlesien and Royal Exchange, La Petite is there . . .'

Another bout of drilling deafened George Dewberry. He looked about him for some way of escape but he was hemmed in by cars on both sides.

'. . . As they go under the mile and a quarter gate, it's

Solomon's Seal from L'Arlesien and Royal Exchange, and Bright Bonfire moving up. Then comes La Petite, behind La Petite is Hard Bitten, Trefoil, Lapsus Linguae, Tirnanoge and Sepulchre. Solomon's Seal setting the pace now . . .'

George Dewberry waited resignedly for the drilling to stop. An irate hooting from behind reminded him of his duty to move up. The road works were now only twenty yards away.

'. . . With a mile to race now, it's still Solomon's Seal two lengths clear of L'Arlesien, then a group of horses including La Petite, Royal Exchange, Hard Bitten, Trefoil, Chemotaxis, Bright Bonfire, Sepulchre is there, Lapsus Linguae, Magistrate moving up on the outside and Battlewagon . . .'

'Yippee!' yelled George Dewberry. Again, an angry hooting brought him back to the Kingston Bypass.

'. . . At the top of the hill, with three quarters of a mile still to go, racing lefthandedly round the bend it's Royal Exchange, Royal Exchange from Bright Bonfire, Chemotaxis and La Petite, the favourite, going well at this stage. Beginning the descent of Tattenham Hill . . .'

The nearest workman leaned determinedly upon his drill and remained there, as though he wanted to finish the job and go home.

'. . . Coming round Tattenham Corner and turning into the straight with four furlongs to go, it's still Royal Exchange from Chemotaxis and Bright Bonfire, La Petite fourth, Sepulchre fifth, Battlewagon in sixth place, Lapsus Linguae making a move there. Passing the three furlong marker it's Bright Bonfire now. Bright Bonfire from Royal Exchange, La Petite improving on the rails and Chemotaxis just showing in fourth place! And now it's Chemotaxis who's come up into the lead! Chemotaxis, La Petite still going easily, Bright Bonfire under pressure, with Battlewagon going very well on the stands side! Two furlongs from home and it's La Petite showing clear of Chemotaxis and Battlewagon! The race is between these three now! Here comes the favourite to make her run, it's La Petite in the lead, will she be the first filly to win the Derby for fifty years! It's La Petite *striding* clear now but here comes Battlewagon to take up the challenge! Inside the final furlong and La Petite is drawing away from Battlewagon! Lapsus Linguae finishing very fast behind them, Chemotaxis dropped right out of it! A hundred yards to go and it's La Petite but Battlewagon is putting in a final burst ... It's going to be a desperate finish for the Derby! Fifty yards to go and it's the two greys, La Petite and Battlewagon there's nothing between them and at the *line* ...'

The workman who had perpetrated the ultimate, the inevitable spasm of drilling which drowned out the finish of the Derby put down his drill and walked over to George Dewberry's car.

'Who won it, mate?'

*   *   *

On the racecourse the thunderous cheering which signalled the finish of the Derby had died away and there was no sound except the mating calls of the bookmakers betting on the result of the photograph.

The Bodger stood looking still at the course where the horses had passed by a few moments before. He knew that on his deathbed his final memory would be of the last furlong of this Derby. Now he understood why people who knew nothing of racing had one bet a year, on the Derby; now he knew why that faraway look had come into Josh's eyes whenever he talked of the Derby; and now he could sympathise with a man who sold all he owned and sent his wife and children out to work for the sake of owning a Derby winner.

Looking down to his right, The Bodger noticed that Julia had gouged four deep nailmarks in her handbag and that tears were still running down Melanie's cheeks. To his left The Bodger saw that at some time during the race Poggles in his agony had removed his top-hat and torn off the brim.

Meanwhile, even the bookmakers had fallen silent as they waited to know whether or not La Petite had been beaten. The bravest hearts amongst them could not help wetting their lips nervously, and wiping the palms of their hands on their trousers. This was going to be either the biggest pay-out or the biggest turn-up for the book in their life-times.

'Here is the result of the Derby,' said the loudspeaker. 'First, number seventeen, Battlewagon . . .'

A vast sigh rustled over the racecourse.

'. . . Second, number eighteen, La Petite. Third, number twenty-one, Lapsus Linguae. Distances, a short head, and one length. Officially placed fourth, number ten, Sepulchre.'

The Bodger was the first to rally the team.

'Julie, my darling, now's your big moment. Go and lead in your Derby winner'.

To Poggles, he said; 'Wakey, wakey, Poggles. You've trained a Derby winner. Hadn't you better go and show an interest in him?'

Poggles turned to The Bodger with the dazed look of a sleep-walker and attempted to replace his mutilated top-hat on his head. 'He won it,' he whispered, so low that The Bodger could hardly hear. 'He actually *won* the Derby.'

Looking as cool as though this were a chore she performed twice a week Julia went out on to the course and took hold of Battlewagon's leading rein. As Battlewagon was led in, a roar gathered, mounted, and rolled across the course from the line of naval buses, whose occupants had been on Battlewagon to a man. It was a roar of triumph, and of salute for a brave performance, it was a roar such as Charlemagne's rearguard raised for Roland, a drinks all round, beer money for months, buy the wean a new rattle, roar. But in the unsaddling enclosure itself there was a prolonged, almost embarrassing, silence. Not a smile shone on any face. Even Tommy Sparling looked strained and shocked. The only gesture of congratulation came from Sir Leonard Brotherhood who, pale as marble, pushed through the crush to shake Julia by the hand. The rest of the faces round the rail looked at Battlewagon with expressions of disbelief, as though he were the fabulous unicorn. As Mme Leonie Tourbillon, the owner of L'Arlesien, said: '*C'est la silence de mort,*' and as Poggles said, when he had pulled himself together, 'Brother, you could have heard a tote ticket drop,' and as Julia said, when congratulated by the television interviewer, 'They all looked so *surprised!*'

16

When The Bodger arrived at the Ministry on the day after the Derby, the hall porter rushed out of his cubicle.

'Congratulations, sir! *Congratulations!* To think we had a Derby winner here all the time!'

'Thank you,' The Bodger said briefly. The hall porter was making too much noise too early in the morning. On his way The Bodger looked into George Dewberry's office and was not surprised to see that George Dewberry was not present. When The Bodger had last seen him, George Dewberry was being cared for by a discreet Savoy Hotel management, having enough alcohol running in his veins to anaesthetise a herd of oxen.

The Savoy Hotel had been as surprised as anyone at the result of the Derby. The result had made some adjustments to the table decorations necessary. The chocolate, green and pink favours had had to be hastily removed and Julia's colours substituted. Luckily, red, white and blue were simple colours and once they were provided the party had gone very well. The Bodger was sure that he had enjoyed it, because he could now remember very little about it, except that Poggles and Melanie had left early on.

Beetle King of Arms was waiting in The Bodger's office.

'I thought you were the best person to have this,' he said.

'Why, thank you very much!'

It was the completed Operation Blue Riband medallion. Beetle King of Arms had touched it up to become an accurate portrait of Battlewagon and he had even succeeded in bringing off a good likeness of Tommy Sparling, in racing colours, sitting in the saddle.

'I thought you'd like it.'

'It's terrific!' said The Bodger warmly. 'Thank you very much!'

'How is the horse this morning?'

'I'm just going to find out.'

Poggles sounded tired and depressed.

'I'm glad you rang up, Bodger. I was going to ring you anyway.'

'You sound a little shop-soiled this morning, Poggles?'

'I am. I didn't get to bed until four.'

'Anything wrong?'

'No, nothing wrong but . . .'

'I really rang up to ask how Battlewagon was this morning and perhaps to discuss Ascot . . .'

'Yes.' Poggles seemed to be selecting his words with care. 'Bodger, I don't think there's any point in running Battlewagon again . . .'

'*What* was that? There's nothing wrong with him, is there?'

'He's a little sore, but that's nothing. Bodger, I've got something to tell you about Battlewagon. I don't feel up to explaining it on the telephone. You couldn't come down here now, could you?'

All The Bodger's listlessness had vanished. 'I'll be right down.'

'I shall have to leave for Epsom at noon. We've got King of Winter running in the Coronation Cup but if you came now I should have time to explain things before I go.'

'I'll come right away!'

Poggles was in his office holding a strip of cine film up to the light when The Bodger burst in on him. He was unshaven and had pouches under his eyes.

'What's all the mystery about, Poggles?'

'Sit down, Bodger. Have a large glass of whisky. I've got a lot to tell you.'

'I couldn't face any whisky just now.'

'Never mind, then.' Poggles put down the roll of film. 'Bodger, weren't you absolutely *amazed* yesterday?'

'I was. Flabbergasted is the word.'

'I was more than that. I was afraid of losing my licence. If it had been any other race but the Derby I should have been hauled up in front of the Stewards like a shot. As it is, I'm astonished they didn't send for me. The point is, Bodger, the Stewards may have been satisfied but I wasn't. I *had* to know what happened yesterday. I think we all knew in our heart of hearts here that Battlewagon was *capable* of winning the Derby. He had the breeding and the speed and the stamina, but he didn't seem to have the guts. I used to think he was too polite to win a race. He didn't want to hurt the other horses' feelings. In that case, *why* did he pull it off yesterday, in the Derby of all races?'

'Perhaps he knew that this was the one time when it really mattered.'

'No, it wasn't that. When Melanie and I got back here last night, we got hold of Josh and Tommy Sparling and Jimmy Bones the stable lad and we had a conference. We went over everything Battlewagon had ever done, who he'd raced against, what feed he'd had, what training gallops he'd done, every single thing we could remember about him. It wasn't until we remembered that time when we all thought he'd been nobbled that we began to have a clue. The funny thing is, *you* had the answer all the time, Bodger.

But we just didn't see it. It wasn't until about half past three this morning that we thought of it. It was Melanie, actually, who thought of it.'

'What do you mean, *I* had the answer?'

'I'm coming to that. Cast your mind back to that trial we laid on last autumn when Battlewagon ran so well. Who did he finish next to, and just beat? Glissade, who was sixth in the Oaks. Now think of the Classic Trials Stakes at Thirsk. Who did he finish next to, and just beat? Gladiola, who was second in the Thousand Guineas. Now the Derby yesterday. Who did he finish next to and just beat? La Petite . . .'

'I'm afraid I'm still not with you.'

'Aren't you? Glissade, Gladiola and La Petite. Three *fillies!*'

'Saint Helena of Constantinople, I'm beginning to see what you mean!'

'Yes. There were no fillies in any of his other races. We know, because we've checked through the *Racing Calendar*. What I'm getting at is that he'll only show an interest when there's a filly in the race. He'll always try and run next to her. That was what he did to La Petite yesterday. It was pure *joss* that he happened to have his whiskers in front as they went over the line.'

'Oh my golly,' moaned The Bodger, 'don't say that.'

'It's true, Bodger. Do you realise that if La Petite had not been running in the Derby, our wonder horse would have finished last and not first? Do you realise that if La Petite had had an off day, supposing she'd gone amiss in the paddock and finished last, our lad would have finished last next to her?'

'Poggles, don't pile it on. I can hardly bear to think about it.'

'You remember he used to spend hours just staring into space, what we call looking out to sea? Do you know what he was thinking about all that time? *Sex!* That's why I say you put your finger on the secret when you suggested parading those fillies up and down outside his box. That must have been right up his street! It had a miraculous effect on him, as you saw. It's all he ever thinks about. He's down in the bottom paddock right now – you can go and see him if you want to – just standing there, thinking about it.'

Poggles began to thread the roll of film through a small projector on his desk.

'Just to give you some visual evidence of what I've been saying, I've got this film of the last four furlongs yesterday. It was taken by Tommy Sparling's wife from the grandstand. A newspaper friend of mine got it developed last night for us. It's not very good but it does show what I'm talking about.'

Poggles drew the office curtains, turned a large calendar to the wall to form a screen and started the projector.

There was first a shot of Tommy Sparling on horse-back and then, there was Epsom, there was the field coming round Tattenham Corner, a straggling blur of hooves, horses' heads nodding, and jockeys' caps. In one flash The Bodger was transported back to that incredible moment when he had first picked out Battlewagon in the Derby amongst a ruck of horses.

'I'll stop the film now. It's very small at this distance but there's La Petite and there's Battlewagon. The two greys, you see. La Petite is fourth here and Battlewagon is sixth and they're both beautifully placed. I must say in passing that Tommy rode a beautiful race. Now I'll start the film again. Do you see how he's looking about him? He's looking for her. Now he's found her. He's moving up out of the field, you see. That's Chemotaxis leading now. But here comes La Petite to make her effort. Now she's going away but watch, see how he's not going to let her get away? You see, he's caught up. Now she's trying again. Just look at old Forres Stirling working like a demon! Again she tries and *again* he's up with her! Forres Stirling must have been wondering what the hell was happening! Now here's the finish. As you can see, there was only a whisker in it.'

The film flicked through the gate, the screen went blank. Poggles drew back the curtains.

'Do you believe me, Bodger?'

'Of course, I believe you, Poggles.'

'To win another race with Battlewagon we've first of all got to make sure there's a filly in the same race capable of beating the rest of the field. Then we've got to hope that Battlewagon happens to have his nose in front at the line. If that's the case, then why not dispense with Battlewagon altogether and just have the filly?'

'Yes, I see that. So what do we do now?'

'Sell him for stud duties. He might be worth anything between sixty thousand and a quarter of a million pounds as a stallion. It depends. But I'll handle all that side, if you like.'

'That's a lot of money!'

'Well, I'm telling you, a Derby winner's worth a lot of money. That's why I'm going to break out into a cold sweat at nights for the rest of my life when I think of what might have happened!'

'Can we go and see him?'

Poggles looked at his watch. 'Yes, we've just got time.'

On the way down in the Land Rover The Bodger said:

'You had fifty pounds on him, didn't you? Was that at fifty to one?'

'No, I got a hundred to one.'

'That's five thousand! We all seem to have cleaned up on this.'

'The race itself was worth about thirty-five thousand pounds. Tommy Sparling gets ten per cent . . .'

'And I'd like to give Josh and Jimmy Bones something, too.'

'Oh yes, I'll fix that. Splitting what's left four ways we should each end up with about seven or eight grand. Did you collect your money yesterday?'

'My goodness, yes. I doff my hat to that bookie, though. He paid up without batting an eyelid. He had the money all ready for me.'

'Did you count it?'

'Later.'

'Was it all there?'

'Five hundred in cash and a cheque for the rest. It must have been like opening a vein for him.'

'I shouldn't waste any sympathy on the bookies. They all made a killing yesterday afternoon. Here we are.'

Battlewagon and the donkey Bill had heard the sound of the approaching Land Rover and were waiting at the paddock gate.

'I should really have brought him something,' The Bodger said.

Battlewagon looked at The Bodger as though saying 'O.K. Buster?'

'He's looking very well,' said The Bodger, stroking the horse's nose. 'I'm sorry I haven't brought anything for you, boy.'

'He's a little sore but nothing much otherwise.'

'It's amazing to think that this same horse was the one that came bounding up the track yesterday and caused all those green faces in the winner's enclosure!'

Battlewagon jerked his head up and turned away to look out across the paddock.

'There he goes again,' said Poggles. 'I should leave him to it. One thing, he's going to make the stallion of the century. There's no danger of him not keeping his mind on his work! I've half a mind to keep a couple of shares in him. It will be interesting to see how his progeny turn out.'

Driving back, Poggles said: 'What are your plans now, Bodger? Would you like me to go to Tattersalls later this year and get you a couple of yearlings so that you can start all over again?'

'Oh no, I don't think so . . .'

'Perhaps it would be better if you chose them yourself. If you came to me with a Himalayan yak, told me it was by Hyperion and you wanted it trained for the Derby, I'd do it, Bodger, after what's happened!'

'Thank you, Poggles, but I don't think I'll try again. I've been thinking. I've come to the conclusion that I'm not really a racing man at heart. I don't think my nerves are strong enough. It's been a fascinating experience but I think I'm going to leave it at that. It's been like a weird dream in a lot of ways.'

The Bodger remembered the morning gallops, the days at the racecourse, the roar of the ring, the flamboyant racing silks, Isinglass's whisky, Poggles scratching his head over his forfeit forms, the day Elsie took the hurdle and left him behind, Josh hissing through his teeth as he groomed a horse, the stable lads' jokes, the furore of the Derby and Battlewagon's ears pricked as he went for the line. As he had said, it had been like a weird dream, an excursion into another world.

'If you ever feel like changing your mind, you know where to come.'

'I know. But I don't think I will. I'd like to say good-bye to everybody.'

'There's nobody here. Josh is up on the gallops. Melanie and Davey are at Epsom and that reminds me, I ought to be going soon myself, Bodger.'

'I mustn't keep you.'

'Well . . . Good-bye, Bodger.'

'Good-bye, Poggles. I'll look for you the next time I go to a race-meeting.'

'Good. Remember, if you ever feel like changing your mind . . .'

* * *

The Bodger had one more duty to perform before the subject of Operation Blue Riband was closed.

'Jim,' he said, 'you remember I said I'd let you know about Blue Riband?'

'Yes?' The Bodger sensed Jim Sewter's ears going to action stations.

'If you want to know what *really* happened, listen . . .'

After The Bodger's first few sentences, Jim Sewter said: 'Just a minute, let me get a pencil.'

When The Bodger had finished, Jim Sewter said: 'Bodger, you wouldn't be pulling my leg by any chance, would you?'

'Now Jim, you know me. When have I ever pulled your leg?'

'This is all Gospel truth and all for the record?'

'Every word.'

'*Right*. Then hold on to your hat . . .'

As The Bodger put down his telephone he remembered

that he ought to congratulate Bert Beattle and Admiralty Archie on their prescience in the Derby; they had picked two of the first three horses and The Bodger had no doubt that if the information Poggles had deduced since the race had been available to Admiralty Archie before the race, he would have named all three.

'You fooled us good and proper, Bodger,' said Bert Beattle. 'Though I still say you didn't tell us everything about that horse of yours.'

'We didn't know everything about him ourselves. What have you got Archie on now?'

'The refitting and maintenance scheme. And we've achieved a break-through!'

'How?'

'If we assume that the Navy has only *one* ship, which *never* goes to sea, then all our problems are solved. It's too simple. In that way you can work out a perfect manning, drafting, refitting, and docking cycle. Everybody knows where they are.'

'One ship which never goes to sea? You mean, what the farmers call zero grazing?'

'Exactly. Only in this case the technical branches like to think of it as Total Maintenance. The work study boys are all for it, too. They call it Planned Immobility.'

'It sounds all right,' said The Bodger. 'One ship which never goes to sea sounds like the matelot's idea of heaven!'

*　　　*　　　*

The press reaction to The Bodger's release about Operation Blue Riband exceeded even The Bodger's expectations. When the story appeared in the morning editions, the country blinked, and then gave one concerted hoot of laughter. The revelation that Operation Blue Riband, about which so many pompous words had been spoken and written, was nothing more than the plan to train and run Battlewagon (now a famous horse) to win the Derby struck the nation squarely on its funny-bone. A *Times* fourth leader speculated on the last occasion when the Senior Service had conspired so successfully to hoodwink the nation and concluded that it had not happened since the time of Samuel Pepys. The *Daily Disaster* published a front page picture of Julia leading Battlewagon in after the Derby, under the headline WE'VE BEEN HAD. Cartoonists in all newspapers broke out fresh boxes of pencils and called loudly for more paper. The Sixth Sea Lord was warmly clapped into lunch at his club and when the Parliamentary Secretary to the Ministry of Political Warfare rose to make his explanatory statement to the Commons he was greeted by Opposition cat-calls of 'Six to four the field!' whereupon the House, according to *Hansard*, 'was convulsed'. Operation Blue Riband became a national joke.

Meanwhile, the author of the joke received a note from Admiral Gilpin. 'The subject of Operation Blue Riband, so-called, may now be considered closed as far as this Department is concerned. The Sixth Sea Lord and I would be pleased if you and Mrs Badger would dine with us tomorrow night. 7.30 for 8, Claridges, black tie.'

Also on The Bodger's desk, received in that morning's mail, was a postcard of some palm trees upon a desolate beach. It was post-marked Christmas Island and was from The Tatler and Bystander, 'Having a bloody awful time,' it said 'Wish you were here.'

The Bodger flicked the postcard across the office, tilted back his chair and settled his feet on the desk. It looked as though all parts in the Department of Naval Public Relations were taking an even strain at last.

The telephone rang.

'Bodger,' said Jim Sewter, 'there's a report that some Wrens have been had up for running a call-girl racket in the Isle of Wight . . .'

A Dangerous Knowing